𝕲he Pomegranates

and Other

Modern Italian Fairy Tales

ODDLY MODERN FAIRY TALES
Jack Zipes, *Series Editor*

Oddly Modern Fairy Tales is a series dedicated to publishing unusual literary fairy tales produced mainly during the first half of the twentieth century. International in scope, the series includes new translations, surprising and unexpected tales by well-known writers and artists, and uncanny stories by gifted yet neglected authors. Postmodern before their time, the tales in *Oddly Modern Fairy Tales* transformed the genre and still strike a chord.

Cristina Mazzoni, editor *The Pomegranates and Other Modern Italian Fairy Tales*

Hermynia zur Mühlen *The Castle of Truth and Other Revolutionary Tales*

Andrei Codrescu, editor *Japanese Tales of Lafcadio Hearn*

Michael Rosen, editor *Workers' Tales: Socialist Fairy Tales, Fables, and Allegories from Great Britain*

Édouard Laboulaye *Smack-Bam, or The Art of Governing Men: Political Fairy Tales of Édouard Laboulaye*

Gretchen Schultz and Lewis Seifert, editors *Fairy Tales for the Disillusioned: Enchanted Stories from the French Decadent Tradition*

Walter de la Mare, with an introduction by Philip Pullman *Told Again: Old Tales Told Again*

Naomi Mitchison, with an introduction by Marina Warner *The Fourth Pig*

Peter Davies, compiler; edited by Maria Tatar *The Fairies Return: Or, New Tales for Old*

Béla Balázs *The Cloak of Dreams: Chinese Fairy Tales*

Kurt Schwitters *Lucky Hans and Other Merz Fairy Tales*

𝔗he Pomegranates

and Other

Modern Italian Fairy Tales

Edited, translated, and with

an introduction by Cristina Mazzoni

PRINCETON UNIVERSITY PRESS   *Princeton and Oxford*

Published by Princeton University Press
41 William Street, Princeton, New Jersey 08540
6 Oxford Street, Woodstock, Oxfordshire OX20 1TR

press.princeton.edu

Library of Congress Cataloging-in-Publication Data

Names: Mazzoni, Cristina, 1965– editor, translator.
Title: The pomegranates and other modern Italian fairy tales /
    edited, translated, and with an introduction by Cristina Mazzoni.
Description: Princeton : Princeton University Press, 2021. |
    Series: Oddly modern fairy tales | Includes bibliographical
    references and index.
Identifiers: LCCN 2021000858 | ISBN 9780691199788 (paperback ;
    acid-free paper) | ISBN 9780691224657 (ebook)
Subjects: LCSH: Fairy tales—Italy. | Shapeshifting. | Folk literature,
    Italian—Translations into English. | BISAC: FICTION /
    Fairy Tales, Folk Tales, Legends & Mythology | LITERARY
    COLLECTIONS / European / Italian
Classification: LCC GR176 .P66 2021 | DDC 398.20945—dc23
LC record available at https://lccn.loc.gov/2021000858

British Library Cataloging-in-Publication Data is available

Editorial: Anne Savarese and James Collier
Production Editorial: Sara Lerner
Text and Cover Design: Pamela L. Schnitter
Production: Erin Suydam
Publicity: Alyssa Sanford and Amy Stewart
Copyeditor: Jennifer Harris

Cover art by Andrea Dezsö

This book has been composed in Adobe Jenson Pro and Luminari

Printed on acid-free paper. ∞

Printed in the United States of America

10 9 8 7 6 5 4 3 2 1

■ Contents

■ List of Illustrations

The Pomegranates

and Other

Modern Italian Fairy Tales

■ Introduction

A handsome youth emerges from a pig's body and three lovely women step out of the rind of pomegranates; soot, animal skin, and vegetable peel are shed to reveal beauty beyond compare; healthy young people become as light as feathers and are carried off by the wind, or grow as heavy as lead and sink into the earth; Catholic saints acquire the appearance and skills of magical helpers—metamorphosis, at the heart of the fairy-tale genre from its very beginning, moves the modern Italian fairy tales collected in this volume. Sometimes the metamorphosis is quite literal and complete: a man turns into a lion, into a dove, into an ant. Sometimes the change is only partial: peach-smooth skin becomes green and scaly as a snake's, a little girl's eyes are made unnaturally, awesomely bright. Other times the transformation resides in the eye of the beholder, who was previously unable to see beyond the veil of dirt or fur or comprehend the inert nature of a wooden doll. More hidden still are the changes that occur within, as when a self-absorbed princess learns about manners if not about compassion, a melancholy prince finds joy in living again, a complacent young woman discovers the transformative power of gratitude—but she also discovers what happens to those who are thankless toward their protector, even if it is the all-loving mother of God. Personal change unites all the tales collected in the present volume and, more than that, personal change allows each of their narratives to unfold. The story of the murderous pig prince would hold little interest without his transformation into a man thanks to the gentleness of his third bride; and if the kind sister's good character were not rewarded with the ability to produce a pearl with every word she says, this heroine would continue to be abused by her relatives, and no story about her would be told.

Political, social, and cultural change also marks the historical time when the tales in this collection were published in Italy, between 1875 and 1914. Very many small states were transformed into a single large one, not without considerable bloodshed; regional identities were painfully turning into a national one; speakers of dialects were becoming speakers of Italian; listeners to stories were changing into readers thereof; out of a solid literary corpus intended for adults a new genre had sprouted, that of literature written expressly for children. The political unification of Italy had been announced in 1861 (with Rome added in 1870, and some Italian cities only decades later), but the inhabitants of the Italian peninsula had not by that time yet acquired a sense of national belonging, much less the certainty of being Italian. "Italy has been made," writer and politician Massimo d'Azeglio is often quoted as saying, "and now it is time to make Italians." In the absence of magical potions or spells, practical measures had to be taken to effect full unification, but disseminating a sense of national identity to subjects who identified with a region instead was difficult in a nation that was for the most part unable to read and write. Nor did Italians share a common language: in 1861, only a small fraction of Italians, 2.5 percent, could read and write in the national language, and standard Italian at the time was experienced by most as a foreign tongue (Boero and De Luca, p. 11). Mandatory schooling was instituted, then, to impel the transformation of a variety of dialects into a shared language, and of an illiterate people into one able to read and write. The growth of schools led to the increased production of textbooks and other readings appropriate to young audiences—and books for children published in these years, therefore, had a clear educational purpose.

Whether through the reading of books or through oral transmission, there was a sense that "Italian-ness" might be achieved through exposure to regional cultures other than one's own. With this goal in mind, what could be more enjoyable, about regional cultures, and more easily shared, than folk and fairy tales? Many such texts were collected and published primarily in the decades following the Italian unification, in a two-pronged effort that would not only spread information about each region across the peninsula but also preserve through print those vulnerable regional identities that were believed to now be at risk because of the unification. Early examples of these publications in the field of folklore were Vittorio Imbriani's volumes of Florentine and Milanese folk tales and Giuseppe Pitrè's collection from Sicily—the latter, a contribution to the gathering and preservation of folklore that, for its sheer size and range, and for how accurately it reflects Sicilian folk traditions, has been described as "more important than the Grimms' tales" (Zipes, p. 16). Both Imbriani and Pitrè employed ethnological methods, carefully avoiding personal interventions and painstakingly recording the oral narratives as they heard them from their informants— who were almost exclusively women (as was also the case of folktale informants in other European countries, such as the Grimms' in Germany). Both Imbriani and Pitrè aimed at preserving with their work the traditional, individual culture of each region they studied, a culture that they believed risked extinction in the newly unified Italian nation. Published in 1870 and recently translated into

English are the tales gathered from peasant women in Sicily by the Swiss fairy-tale collector Laura Gonzenbach. Her contribution was different: collected in the informants' Sicilian language, these narratives were then published in Gonzenbach's German translation. Largely for this reason, their reception was lukewarm at best: Pitrè praised them but also inveighed against the fact that these Sicilian stories were being published in a distant and foreign tongue.

It is out of the volumes compiled by these and other nineteenth-century folklorists that Italo Calvino several decades later conjured up his own *Italian Folktales* (1956), transforming what were by then obscure ethnological texts from the previous century into the first collection of Italian tales appealing to the general public. That Calvino's should be the earliest popular Italian collection of fairy tales seems like an especially late event considering that the oldest printed European stories that we can easily recognize as fairy tales come from Italy. In sixteenth-century Venice, Giovan Francesco Straparola wrote seventy-five short narratives, *The Pleasant Nights*; most are realistic short stories, but several of them revolve around magic and include the earliest versions of such classics as Perrault's "Puss in Boots" and "Donkey Skin." Almost a hundred years later, in Naples, Giambattista Basile published *The Tale of Tales, or Entertainment for Little Ones*, made up of fifty fairy tales written in a baroque Neapolitan tongue, addressed to a courtly adult audience, and including the oldest Cinderella, Hansel and Gretel, Sleeping Beauty, and Snow White tales in Europe. The Italian fairy-tale tradition slowed considerably following this rambunctious start, and after the intermezzo of Carlo Gozzi's eighteenth-century theatrical fairy tales (some of which have been made famous through opera: *Turandot* and *The Love of the Three Oranges*), it picks up again in the second half of the nineteenth century, with the stories gathered by folklorists or invented by writers. The tales in the present collection are representative of the tales published in Italy in the late nineteenth and early twentieth centuries in that they include translations from the French; more or less literary variants of common folkloric types—identified by scholars through the ATU Index of Tale Types, which catalogues hundreds of different tale cycles; and more original and eclectic literary tales that combine motifs from different tale types without being recognizable variants of a single one. This abundance and variety of published fairy tales was not unique to Italy during this time period; on the contrary, the second half of the nineteenth century especially witnessed a fairy-tale boom throughout Europe, most famously expressed in the Grimm brothers' project of German nation-building through their *Children and Household Tales*. Not unlike their Italian counterparts, the better-known Grimms believed that their folk tales would help to provide the shared culture necessary for the birth of a cohesive nation. Thus, although the Grimms' first edition in 1812 was addressed to scholars, the popular success of their collection led the brothers to repackage their book as family edutainment. In the publishing trajectory of the Grimm brothers' work, we also see some of the changes in the fairy tales' readership more generally: from sophisticated adults to a more general and increasingly young audience.

In Italy, however, it wasn't until Calvino's *Italian Folktales* that we find a popular book of fairy tales believed to embody a national storytelling tradition and appealing to a wide readership. Calvino draws several of his tales from the collection of Italian folk stories *Novelline popolari italiane* (Popular Italian short stories, 1875), by classical philologist Domenico Comparetti, of which three volumes were planned but only one published. Like Calvino, and unlike the other folk-tale collectors of his era, Comparetti includes stories from many regions of Italy, instead of focusing on a single area like Pitrè, Imbriani, and Gonzenbach. Furthermore, and again like Calvino, Comparetti translates his tales from the local dialect of each region into standard Italian, which he calls "the common language" ("la lingua commune," p. v). Both Calvino and Comparetti, then, were willing to transform each tale's original language—and in so doing sacrifice its "purity"—for the sake of producing an edition readable and enjoyable by all Italians even as they preserved what they saw as the essence of each tale. Comparetti's tales, considerably less literary than Calvino's, follow the cadence of spoken speech, with ungrammatical switches between verb tenses, the frequent use of "and" to start a new sentence, and phatic communication with the audience especially at the end of a tale: "Go check," the narrator invites his audience at the end of the pig prince's tale, "because the dances have begun." This type of interactive ending is typical of orally transmitted stories, and it is also present in some literary fairy tales—forming one of the many threads that link literary fairy tales with their oral counterparts. Thus, the narrator in Luigi Capuana's Cinderella-like story "Sunbeam" ends his tale with the bittersweet statements: "That evening the wedding was celebrated, and the prince and Little Charcoal lived a long and happy life. While we instead stay here and grind our teeth."

Comparetti's tales translated in this volume connect the Italian folk-tale tradition gathered in the late nineteenth century with the literary fairy tales that preceded it in print: "The King's Son, A Pig" is clearly a version of Straparola's sixteenth-century "The Pig Prince"—both classified as ATU 425A, The Animal Bridegroom, and related to the "Beauty and the Beast" tales; Comparetti's "Bad Pumpkin" belongs to the same type as Perrault's "Donkey Skin" (present in this volume through Collodi's translation), Straparola's "Doralice," and Basile's "The She-Bear" (ATU 510B, The Persecuted Heroine, Donkey Skin); and "The Pomegranates" is an instance of the Mediterranean tale type of The Three Oranges (ATU 408)—first printed in Basile's "The Three Citrons" and also appearing, in this volume, in Gabriele D'Annunzio's "Song of the Bloodied Ricotta." The presence of two or more versions of similar stories and the recurrence of fairy-tale motifs in this volume is meant to emphasize both the impressive persistence of certain narrative elements and how the changed details make a difference. Take, for example, Deledda's and Gozzano's tales by the same name, "The Three Talismans"—both versions of ATU 563, The Knapsack, the Hat, and the Horn. Deledda's three brothers, in a tale firmly anchored in Sardinian folklore, receive their talismans from local fairies as recompense for their kindness; whereas in the similar literary version by Gozzano, it is the young men's father who bequeaths them the magical objects at his death; and while in Deledda's version the antagonists are politically powerful prelates, explicitly described as connected to the Inquisition, it is with a cunning princess that Gozzano's single protagonist must contend—he does not marry her, as one might expect, choosing instead a fellow village woman, but in Deledda's story there is no marriage at all at the end of the tale.

At the same time as oral versions of classic tales appeared in volumes by folklore scholars such as Comparetti, canonical French fairy tales were being published in Italian translation. The most enduring and influential of these were by the Tuscan children's author Carlo Lorenzini, best-known as Collodi and famous the world over for his children's novel *Pinocchio* (1883). Just a few years before writing the beloved puppet's adventures, in 1876, Collodi was commissioned to translate a French anthology from 1853, made up of fairy tales from the previous two centuries. This book was titled, simply, *Contes de fées*, which Collodi translated literally as *I racconti delle fate* instead of the more Italian "fiabe." And although this very set of tales had already appeared in Italian in 1867, in a translation by writer and journalist Cesare Donati, it is Collodi's eponymous titles from 1876 that endured. Perrault's unforgettable "Petit chaperon rouge" ("Little Red Riding Hood") and "Barbe-bleue" ("Bluebeard") are still known today in Italy with Collodi's "Cappuccetto Rosso" and "Barba-blu," and not with Donati's "Berrettina Rossa" and "Barba Turchina." Collodi's brief preface to his translation is often quoted for the insight it provides into this author's ambiguous and often downright contradictory translating practices:

> In translating these *Fairy Tales* into Italian I tried, to the best of my abilities, to remain faithful to the French text. Freely paraphrasing them would have felt somewhat of a sacrilege. In any event, here and there I allowed myself some slight variants, in terms of word choice, sentence rhythm, and idiomatic expressions; and I wanted to make a note of this fact right from the start, so as to avoid comments, sudden astonished reactions, and grammatical or lexical misgivings. A sin that is confessed is half forgiven: let that be true for me. [p. 5; my translation into English]

Collodi does in fact modify and thoroughly domesticate the French tales, for his audience is the Italian middle and working classes rather than French courtiers: in place of Perrault's aristocratic tone, Collodi employs a language close to the spoken word and to his own Tuscan speech; and the philosophical morals that Perrault appends at the end of his tales assume in Collodi a more practical and bour-geois attitude. Collodi's beautiful translation of Perrault's "Donkey Skin," for example, simplifies both the content and the style of the original, even as some of the French author's statements are ren-dered with exquisitely Tuscan tones: the king and queen are de-scribed by Collodi as "due anime in un nocciolo" (literally "two souls in a fruit pit," which I have translated here as "two peas in a pod"), whereas Perrault had simply said that they "lived in perfect union" ("vivaient dans une union parfaite"); and if Perrault prosaically states that life's ups and downs ("les vicissitudes de la vie") extend to kings as well as to their subjects, for the Tuscan Collodi such reversals of fortune are roof tiles ("tegoli") that fall on the heads of kings as well as their subjects. Also translated here because of its influence on Italian tales from this time is "The Fairies," included in every edi-tion of Collodi's book since 1944 although it is actually absent from his original collection (and from the 1853 French book he trans-lated). It was instead turned into Italian by Collodi's friend Yorick (the pen name of Pietro Coccoluto Ferrigni) in his 1891 translation of Perrault. We see another version of this same tale in one of Gozzano's stories included in this volume, "The Dance of the Gnomes," which, like Perrault's "The Fairies," belongs to ATU 480, The Kind and the Unkind Girls. A cruel twist on its central motif of sisters' rivalry appears in Perodi's "Lavella's Stepmother"—where the sister who, according to the logic of the tale, dies a painful death at the hand of Providence, has no other fault than that of being ugly and favored by her evil mother.

Both the folk tales gathered by ethnologists and the translations from beloved volumes of the French *contes de fées* influenced the creation of new literary fairy tales by late nineteenth-century professional writers working to a greater or lesser extent within the parameters of the oral folk-tale genre. Fairy tales are notoriously difficult to define: despite their name, they often have no fairies; they may be published in print or orally transmitted, have a named author or be anonymous, feature psychologically flat characters or ones filled with intense emotions; most fairy tales are short and have a happy ending—but not every single one; all have magic, but this element may be defined in a variety of ways. The tales collected in this volume all have a named author, but while some are original and free-standing creations, others were collected from oral sources. Regardless of their origin, these tales all share several traits: the central role of magic in a short narrative where the protagonists rise from rags to riches or regain their lost high status; villains are punished and virtues such as generosity and kindness, as well as resourcefulness and shrewdness, are rewarded; and a happily ever after that often includes a wedding closes the plot. Some of the authors in this volume drew explicitly from regional folk stories, disseminating these otherwise inaccessible narratives through a transformation of the local dialect into standard Italian. In addition to Comparetti, this is the case with Gabriele D'Annunzio, who in 1886 published in a literary magazine two short fairy tales from his home region of Abruzzo, "The Doves" and "The Song of the Bloodied Ricotta," translating them from the Abruzzese and, with an ethnological move, even specifying in a subtitle their city of origin—S. Eusanio del Sangro and Aquila, respectively. D'Annunzio's regular literary production is marked by a fascination with Abruzzese beliefs and legends, which he incorporates in his otherwise realistic fiction; a well-known example of this is his verse play, *The Daughter of Iorio* (1903), which includes proverbs, rituals, and traditional rhymes from Abruzzo. "The Doves" and "The Song of the Bloodied Ricotta" read like folk tales and follow the simple vocabulary and paratactic structure of orally gathered stories: they could easily have appeared in Comparetti's own volume. Almost twenty years later, D'Annunzio published a much longer fairy tale, titled "The Borea's Daughter." This story shares with "The Song of the Bloodied Ricotta" elements of ATU 408, The Three Oranges, including a dark-skinned impostor bride who is explicitly racialized in the older tale as "that ugly Saracen," and more generically disparaged in the later tale because dark skinned. "The Borea's Daughter" is also as an example of the Rapunzel tale type, ATU 310, The Maiden in the Tower, with its powerful mother figure and captor, a beautiful maiden's imprisonment in a tower, the surreptitious entrance of a prince, the lovers' treacherous escape. "The Borea's Daughter," unlike D'Annunzio's previous two narratives, bears the stamp of what this author became known for in the twentieth century: the exuberant style of Italy's foremost decadent writer, a style evident from the very first paragraph for its poetic lists and rarefied atmosphere (a court made up of wise knights, monks, astrologers, and alchemists), antiquated words ("vecchiezza" for old age, instead of the more standard "vecchiaia"), and obscure cultural references (the medieval compendium of mythological gem-lore known as the Lapidary of Bishop Marbod).

Another writer whose fiction is inflected by a close bond to her home region is Grazia Deledda, the only Italian woman to have received the Nobel prize in literature. Her most famous works are realistic novels and short stories intimately tied to the island of Sardinia: these otherwise realistic texts contain multiple references to local beliefs and folklore. In addition to fiction, Deledda wrote ethnological articles and recorded a number of legends from her region. These were written with clear authorial interventions, starting with the fact that, like D'Annunzio, she published them in standard Italian rather than in the Sardinian language in which they were told—thus making them readable outside their region of origin. Some of Deledda's folklore-inspired texts were introduced as legends by Deledda herself but read today much like fairy tales, including "The Three Talismans" and, above all, "Our Lady of Good Counsel." The latter is by far the longest among Deledda's tales of magic. It can be said to loosely belong to the Persecuted Heroine tale type (ATU 510B): an incestuous male relative's desire impels the protagonist's flight from home, as for Perrault's "Donkey Skin" (with whom it also shares the presence of a fairy godmother of sorts) and Comparetti's "Bad Pumpkin"; also like these tales, the narrative is ultimately resolved by the transformed and thus unrecognizable heroine's timely use of her wits. Unlike the majority of fairy tales, however—which at most speak of gods and goddesses, like "Donkey Skin," and not of the Judeo-Christian god or Catholic saints—Deledda's identifies the heroine's helper as Mary, the mother of Jesus in the Christian scriptures. In her representation as Our Lady of Good Counsel (a reference to a miraculous medieval fresco of Virgin and Child in Genazzano, near Rome), Mary appears in this tale as a blend of fairy and Queen of Heaven, a Catholic intercessor from the spiritual realm and a magical creature with practical powers over nature.

The seamless blend of magic and Catholicism is not unique to "Our Lady of Good Counsel," for it is also central to many tales by the prolific Tuscan author Emma Perodi. Her *Novelle della nonna* (Grandmother's tales, 1893) comprises forty-five fairy stories set in the Casentino region, in eastern Tuscany, during the Middle Ages. Despite certain anachronisms, such as the occasional appearance of corn fields in the countryside, Perodi's tales include numerous historical references, and her writing effectively evokes a medieval atmosphere with haughty feudal nobility and serfs who know their place, herbal poisons and aristocratic jousts, and a magically inflected Catholicism that does not distinguish between fairies and angels, between saints and magical helpers—not to mention the devil and the deadly pacts he makes with desperate humans. Perodi's tales are not derived from the oral tradition, despite their many debts to it, but instead are the author's own creation; these stories draw from noncanonical genres including the gothic, popular legend, and literature for children, but are entirely the invention of an author who knew folk tales so intimately as to produce works that were new yet sounded traditional. All the tales are told within a narrative frame reproducing an oral setting around the hearth of a Tuscan, late nineteenth-century family, whose supposedly real-life events we read about in between the fantastic tales told by the family's elderly matriarch, Nonna Regina. The latter is a fictional character who perfectly embodies contemporary ethnologists' paradigmatic informant: she is elderly, female, and peasant. But Nonna Regina is an idealized sort of peasant, and her cultured and refined language allows Perodi's tales to reach a wide audience extending beyond her own region to all of newly united Italy. Catholic belief blends easily in Perodi's work with fairy-tale magic and folk superstition, as it does in Deledda's. Thus, for example, Lavella, who like Snow White is the object of her stepmother's murderous intentions, is consoled by her fairy-like guardian angel, who saves her life with a miraculous ointment; the Madonna's veil, much like the rosary in Deledda's "Our Lady of Good Counsel," not only protects Lisa from the devil's assaults but also allows her to magically heal the sick and control the forces of nature; in both of these tales, the ultimate antagonist is the devil himself; and it was Saint John the

Evangelist (who is oddly confused, in this book, with John the Baptist, by being described as Herod's victim and represented with a decapitated head) who sent the feisty white mule that rescues the Abbess Sofia, kills her enemies, and lives a supernaturally long life. Sofia, like Straparola's Costanza and Basile's Belluccia, is a gender-bending heroine who, in the absence of a capable brother, has acquired manly skills with horses and weapons in order to defend her family, and whose fearlessness undermines the stereotype of the passive fairy-tale female protagonist.

In addition to featuring resilient and clever female characters, Deledda's and Perodi's fairy tales explicitly name Gospel figures, historical personages, and the real-world locations where they unfold, along with the cultural information connected to them—be it, in Deledda, the Sardinian village of Nurri with its local witches (*janas*) and typical flute-like musical instrument (*leoneddas*); or, in Perodi, the Casentino area in Tuscany, whose nobility hunted with falcons, practiced jousting, and went to war against neighboring Florence. Luigi Capuana, the most steadily productive of modern Italian fairy-tale authors, also sets his literary fairy tales in his native region, the island of Sicily, but his cultural references are more subtle than Deledda's or Perodi's. The first of Capuana's many volumes of fairy tales, *C'era una volta . . . Fiabe* (Once upon a time . . . fairy tales, 1882), made of stories that are overtly indebted to the oral tradition yet remain Capuana's original creations, came out shortly after the publication of his friend Giuseppe Pitrè's massive ethnological work on the folklore of their common home region and is clearly related to it. But although Sicily can be seen in the landscape of Capuana's fairy tales, the fact that they are written in standard Italian and in a very simple style, including the occasional use of Tuscan terms such as "babbo" (father) and "figliolo" (son), reduces the effect of otherness and makes them enjoyable to non-Sicilians as well. Princes and princesses in Capuana's tales are called "Reucci" and "Reginotte," according to a Sicilian usage that appears exclusively in the language of fairy tales—terms that are both odd-sounding and generally understandable to every Italian, thus forming a bridge between Sicilian culture and the world of children across the Italian peninsula. Different from the idealized representation of kings and queens in many canonical fairy tales are Capuana's royal figures, portrayed as capricious and self-centered—much as figures of power and authority are in this author's fiction for adults. Thus, the prince in the Cinderella story titled "Sunbeam" spits on the heroine and kicks her in the stomach for no reason other than he disliked her looks: she has the dark skin of one who works with dirt and soot, and the color of her complexion marks her lower social class (this was also the case with "Donkey Skin," whose dirty dark skin contributes to hiding her identity). That in the end Sunbeam marries the prince who abused her speaks to the strength of her desire for social advancement, from baker to queen. All that the spoiled princess Golden Feather seems to learn from her mistake of mistreating a fairy disguised as a poor old woman is to never again eat salt and pepper—after the fairy, in punishment, turns all of her food and drink into those two condiments. Nothing at all is mentioned in this tale about learning kindness to strangers or comparable teachings.

Like Capuana, Cordelia (the pen name of Virginia Tedeschi Treves, taken from that of King Lear's beloved daughter) wrote and directed periodicals for both children and adults. Her tales translated here are "wordier" than those of everyone else in this collection except D'Annunzio's last one—distant, that is, from the oral tradition, which favored a simple and concise style—and, although like the others they are set in a vaguely medieval era and provide geographical coordinates (Portugal and Japan), these coordinates denote exoticism rather than regionalism. Cordelia's tales make no attempt to capture the cadence of spoken storytelling, and their literary merits are limited, although they are also representative of numerous other fairy tales published during that time. With a tone that is didactic and even at times preachy, Cordelia's "Prince Valorous's Doll" (whose protagonist is melancholy like the prince in "Bad Pumpkin," "Donkey Skin," and "The Borea's Daughter") and "Fiery Eyes" (whose baptismal spell is reminiscent of the Sleeping Beauty cycle) unfold in castles and forests and feature kings and princesses, knights and shepherds, and, of course, fairies. But the tripling that characterizes fairy tales feels in these pages repetitive rather than magical, pedantic instead of incantatory, and the protagonists are unpleasant more than downtrodden—they appear as whiny teenagers more than unjustly persecuted young people, and their transformation into empathetic adults is not really believable even given the suspension of disbelief required by the fairy-tale genre.

Quite different from Cordelia's long-winded fairy tales are the succinct and poetic ones of Guido Gozzano, so whimsical and beautiful and for these reasons appealing even to this day to children and adults alike. Gozzano's narratives unfurl in an imaginary world located outside of geography and history, yet bearing, like the other tales in this volume, the stamp of the European Middles Ages: there are sumptuous castles and mysterious forests, handsome princes and beautiful princesses, righteous kings and queens, unpredictable fairies, dangerous witches, and enduring magic spells of unknown origin. Gozzano's tales fit well within the literary current of *crepuscolarismo*, of which he is considered the most important exponent.

Named after the Italian word for twilight (*crepuscolo*), *crepuscolarismo* is marked by a romantic discontent with the present time and by the quest for another world. Gozzano first published his tales in the children's periodical *Il Corriere dei Piccoli* between 1909 and 1914, with a majority dating from 1911—significantly, the same year that he published his major collection of poetry, *I Colloqui* (Dialogues). Thus, the three helpers in "Goldenfeather and Finestlead" that are named with Latinate, poetic names—pieris (white cabbage butterfly), pappus (dandelion puff), and scarab beetle—appear in Gozzano's work for adults with the same unusual names: "pieride," "achenio," "cetonia." "Goldenfeather and Finestlead" shares its central motif with Capuana's "Golden Feather" (in turn based on George MacDonald's "The Light Princess," 1864), and in the differences between these two stories, both featuring a female protagonist who becomes so light as to float away from home, we see the very differences between the two authors more generally. Where Capuana's protagonist is royal, spoiled, and mean, spellbound as punishment and singlehandedly saved by a brave and kind prince, Gozzano's heroine is as poor as poor gets, with an outer beauty that reflects her inner kindness; her spell has no apparent cause or meaning and it is she who saves a prince—and in saving him, she saves herself. The verses that are regularly repeated in Capuana's version are ominous and vaguely threatening ("With the wind you shall arrive and / With the rain you shall then leave"), whereas those in Gozzano's tale are gentle and contain a soothing promise: "The only one I adore—is Goldenfeather. / O Goldenfeather, / You beautiful child—you will be Queen." Likewise, though Gozzano's "The Three Talismans" repeats the major motifs of Deledda's tale by the same name—three brothers are given three magical objects that lift them from poverty into a life of comfort—it has none of the Sardinian writer's regional inflections. Rather, it features the semilegendary geography of the Fortunate Islands that also appear in "Goldenfeather and Finestlead" as well as in Gozzano's poetry.

Whether or not the Fortunate Islands correspond, as some have wondered, to the archipelago of the Canary Islands in the Atlantic Ocean, their geography in Gozzano's work is magical, otherworldly: it is a place reachable only by magical flight, a place capable of producing wonder-working fruit, a place of utter enchantment. A similar otherworldliness is present in Cordelia's Portugal and Japan—the latter, a land she calls the "Kingdom of the Rising Sun." Despite the clearly stated geographical coordinates, there is no realistic description of these foreign lands in these two authors' tales. Equally unfamiliar to most Italian readers, however, in spite of their specific (and Italian) geographical localities, would have been Deledda's Sardinian landscape, with its fairies called *orgianas*, its ancient and fairy-tale-sounding name of Arborea, and its vivid memories of the Inquisition; Perodi's Tuscan countryside village, with the unusual name of Poppi and intimately tied to the Camaldolese order and its eleventh-century founder by the unusual name of Saint Romuald; Capuana's Sicilian villages and their spoiled and whiny lords; or D'Annunzio's Abruzzi, with its fairy-tale-sounding locations: S. Eusanio del Sangro, Aquila. The magnifying lens that these modern Italian tales place over details that would have been little-known outside their immediate locations and cultures allows the natural to appear as supernatural, the domestic as foreign, real life as the most unrealistic of settings. The stories that are gathered together in this volume share a time period, a language, a nation, and a genre; they are but a minuscule sampling of the astonishingly large number of Italian fairy tales published in the late nineteenth and early twentieth century. Nevertheless, in their multiple transformations, varied styles, and diverse perspectives; in their wide-ranging geographical settings and borrowings from numerous genres; and in their incorporation of local superstitions and transnational religion, they give readers a taste of an era of change and surprise, of adventure and novelty. The vicissitudes of their brave and flawed protagonists, who steadfastly move into unfamiliar and possibly dangerous territories, parallel the movement of a new nation and of its people into their own uncharted history, into becoming one nation and one people with a shared past, with a shared language, and, especially, with shared stories.

Tales

The King's Son, a Pig

Once upon a time, there was a king who had a son. This son looked like a pig by day and a handsome young man by night. Until he turned twenty, he always kept to the back of the palace, and behaved like a human being.

One day, just as he was sitting down at the table to eat, the king felt the palace tremble: it was like an earthquake. The servants went to see what was going on, and in a room they found the pig jumping up and down, and he was jumping so high that he reached all the way up to the ceiling. They asked him what was the matter, and he said that he wanted to find a wife, and he had his eye on the eldest of the miller's three daughters. So, the king sent for the miller and told him that his son wanted to marry one of his daughters and explained to him what his son looked like. In short, he told him everything. And the miller answered that, as far as he was concerned, he was happy about this marriage, so long as his daughter was also happy.

For his daughter, too, the desire to become queen was reason enough to marry even a pig. And so, a banquet was held for the bride and groom, and while they were eating, the pig kept sticking his snout into his bride's plate, but she used her fork to push him back, and she pushed him back so hard that his snout bled. Evening came, and the new queen went to sleep in her bed. At the stroke of midnight, she awoke to the sound of glass shattering and a handsome man entering her room, his face all bloodied. He said to her, "If you had not treated me so poorly, we could have enjoyed our life together. But instead, you will die by my hand." And he took out his sword and killed her.

The next day, the entire court went to say good morning to the bride, but instead found her dead and the entire room covered in blood. After two or three months had gone by, again the palace shook, even harder than the first time. It was the king's son, who wanted to take a wife, and he wanted the second of the miller's daughters. At first, she wavered between yes and no, but then said she was happy to marry the king's son. When they sat down at table to eat, the pig wanted to stick his nose everywhere, but "Zack!" she stabbed his snout with her fork so hard that he was injured.

At night, when she went to bed, things went even worse for her than for her sister, because the young man cut her to pieces. Some five or six months later, the palace again trembled from top to bottom, because the king's son wanted the third of the miller's daughters. And his father gave her to him, saying, "Be careful: when this one is gone, you might as well be seventy years old because you will no longer find a wife to take."

They held the wedding and sat down at table to eat. This third sister was more prudent than the others, and when the pig stuck his snout into her plate, she gently wiped it with a napkin, to help him eat more easily. After they finished eating, they retired to their chambers. At midnight, the most handsome young man in the world arrived in her bedroom. She gave him focaccia to eat, and he remained a handsome young man for the rest of his life. In the morning, everyone thought they would hear funeral bells, but instead they found the bride and groom alive and happy. And so, there were banquets and parties. You should go check, because the dances have begun.

The Pomegranates

There was a king who had a melancholy son who never laughed, and no amusements or distractions could get him to laugh. His father did not know what to do to cheer him up, and one day he had the idea of building three fountains in front of the royal palace, in the square: one that spewed wine, another one oil, and the last one vinegar. Everyone of course crowded to draw from those fountains, and they were constantly bumping into each other, causing ridiculous scenes. But it was all to no avail: the prince looked out the palace window without even the trace of a smile on his face. The wine ran out and so did the vinegar. The oil was about to run out, too, when a little old woman arrived and started filling her small flask, drop by drop. It was taking her a long time, and she was losing patience. From the window, the prince enjoyed watching her, and just to cause trouble, when she had almost finished filling the flask, he took a stone and threw it with such good aim that he broke the flask and started laughing wildly. The old lady angrily turned to him and screamed: "Ah, so now you laugh? Good boy, laugh away, but your life will have no meaning and amount to nothing unless you find the girl made of milk and blood."

These words made him even more melancholy than before. So, he told his father that he wanted to go search for the girl made of milk and blood, just as the old woman had said. He took some money and left. He walked and walked and saw many different cities and many different countries, but he could not find a girl that fit the woman's description.

One morning, he arrived at a forest and began wandering aimlessly. After so much walking, he was thirsty, but could not find water to drink nor a house where he could ask for some. He sat down on the ground, since he really could not go any further, and after he rested a bit, he lifted his eyes and saw a tree with three pomegranates. "Look," he said to himself, "I'll pick one to quench my thirst a little."

So, he picked a pomegranate, opened it, and out jumped a beautiful maiden who was white and red and made of milk and blood. The prince asked her: "Do you want to come and stay with me?"

"Do you have something to eat and to drink?"

"I don't."

"Then I will not stay with you."

And the maiden went back into the pomegranate and onto the tree. The prince picked another pomegranate and opened it and out came another maiden just like the first one. This one, too, asked him if he had something to eat and to drink, and he answered he didn't. So, she went back into the pomegranate like the first one and refused to go with the prince. Then the prince picked the third pomegranate, and after he opened it, another maiden jumped out, made of milk and blood.

"Do you want to come and stay with me?" asked the prince.

"Do you have something to eat and to drink?"

This time the prince answered, "Yes, I do."

"Then I shall come and stay with you."

She told him that a fairy had put a spell on all three maidens and kept them inside those pomegranates. The fairy had entrusted to them a magic wand, a hazelnut, an almond, and a walnut. So, the maiden took all those things with her, waved the magic wand, and cried out, "I want a carriage with horses."

Right away, a beautiful carriage appeared, with horses hitched to it. Then the maiden and the prince climbed into the carriage and left. The fairy came back, and she was an old woman. When she saw the maidens come out of their pomegranates, and realized that there were just two, she asked, "And Caterina? Where is she? Where did she go?"

The other maidens told her all that had happened, and the old woman immediately ran after Caterina. But since Caterina was careful and expected this to happen, she tossed the walnut, and out of the walnut came a chapel, and inside the chapel Caterina was transformed into a priest and the prince into an altar boy.

Now, the old woman entered the chapel and asked: "Have you seen a young woman and a young man pass by?"

"What do you want?" answered the altar boy. "Do you want to attend Mass? The bell is about to toll."

"No! I asked whether you saw a young woman with a young man."

"Ah, maybe you want a blessing?"

And they got the old woman so confused that she turned back. Then the two returned to the carriage, climbed into it, and continued on.

The old woman went back to the place where she had left the two other maidens.

"Maria, did Caterina take the walnut with her?"

"Of course she did."

And so, once again, the old woman set out and followed Caterina. She was about to catch her, but as soon as Caterina saw her, she tossed a hazelnut, and right away a beautiful garden appeared. At the same time, she and the prince were turned into gardeners.

"Would either of you happen to have seen a young woman with a young man?"

"What do you want?" asked the gardener. "Do you want a bunch of roses? Let me go pick some for you."

"Forget about the roses! I am telling you . . ."

"I understand, you want a bunch of acacia flowers. Let me go pick some for you."

And in the end, Caterina and the prince made the old woman so upset that she turned back. Once again, the two started back on their path, while the old woman returned and asked the two other maidens: "Tell me, you two, did Caterina by any chance take with her the almond and the hazelnut?"

"Yes, she took everything with her, even the magic wand."

"Oh, poor me! What am I going to do?"

And she started running again, and she ran and ran. Since she was a fairy, she was extremely fast and almost caught up to them again. But as soon as Caterina saw her, she tossed the almond, and immediately a jagged river appeared. This river looked like it was made of water like any other river, but anyone who swam in it would get cut up by many sharp knives. So, the old woman could not get across. She wavered a bit, and in the end resolved to go into the river and cross it by swimming. But as soon as she was in, the water cut her to pieces and she died. In that very moment, the river disappeared and all of the fairy's enchantments ended. The prince and Caterina turned back to pick up the other two maidens, and they all went to the palace. The prince married Caterina, who was the youngest, and gave the other two as brides to two princes. And thus, the melancholy prince became cheerful, and from that moment on, he never knew melancholy again.

Bad Pumpkin

A king had a wife who suddenly fell ill, and within a few days she was on the brink of death. The king was distraught and never left his wife's bedside.

"Dear wife," he told her, "if you die, I don't want any other woman around. I promise you I will remain a widower and mourn you for as long as I shall live."

But his wife replied: "Dear husband, absolutely not! I don't want you to do that. Since I'm leaving only a daughter behind, you must provide an heir to the throne. So, do take another wife. But only take one who is your equal, and whose finger fits this ring."

As she said this, she took off her wedding ring, gave it to the king, and after a few moments, she died. The king took the ring and, deeply saddened by his wife's death, tossed it into a box inside a chest of drawers and never gave it a second thought. Indeed, he absolutely refused to get married again. In the meantime, the king's daughter, who at her mother's death was about ten years old, grew very fast and became quite beautiful, thanks also to the nurse who had raised her as a baby and took care of her.

One day, when this daughter was about seventeen years old, she opened an old chest of drawers and found the box with the ring her father had tossed there years earlier.

"How lovely it is!" she exclaimed. "How very lovely!"

So, she took it and slipped it onto her finger. To her surprise, it fit as if it had been custom made for her. Bursting with joy, the girl immediately ran to her father, crying out, "Father! Father! Look at the lovely little ring I found! See how well it fits me?"

"Dear daughter," the king replied, "that is your poor mother's ring, rest her soul. Now I must tell you what she said when she gave it to me. She told me that I had to marry a woman who was my equal and whose finger fit this ring. Therefore, dear daughter, you must be my bride."

The princess was horrified by such an evil proposal. Then the king began to caress her, speaking words to her that were not a father's words, but a lover's. Ashamed and dismayed, the princess barely escaped from her father's grip and ran straight to her nurse. With tears rolling down her cheeks, she told her nurse what had just happened.

"Don't be afraid, my girl," the nurse said, "but don't argue with your father, either. Listen to me, and I will advise you well. You must promise to marry him, as long as he gives you a silk dress the color of air, studded with the stars of the sky. There isn't a dress like that in the entire world, and so you will not be obliged to keep your promise."

The king's daughter liked that idea, so she went to her father and requested the dress. The king did not know how to satisfy her because it seemed impossible that such a fabric even existed. He then called his trusted servant and told him: "Tonino! Take some money, take the horses, take whatever you need, and search for a silk dress the color of the air studded with the stars of the sky. Pay whatever it costs! But be sure that you don't come back without it."

The servant thought his master had gone mad, but didn't dare argue with him. Instead, he mounted his horse with a bag full of golden coins, and off he went across the world, seeking this unusual dress. But wherever he went, he could not find a dress like the one the king wanted. Then, one day, after six months of useless travel, the servant entered a city where many Jews lived. He immediately went to a fabric shop and said to the merchant: "Would you happen to have silk fabric for a dress like this and that?"

The Jewish merchant answered: "Well, of course I have it. I even have the most beautiful one in the world."

You can imagine the servant's joy! The merchant sold him the fabric for twenty gold coins, and, without delay, the servant set back on his path toward the king.

As soon as the servant arrived at the palace with the dress, the king had his daughter summoned. He said to her: "Here is what you wanted. Therefore, it is now time for the wedding." The girl collapsed to the floor at that news. As soon as she could get away, she ran to her nurse to tell her that the dress had been found. The nurse, who was never short of alternative plans, said: "Don't be dismayed, dear girl. There is a remedy for everything, except for death. You must tell your father that you are not happy with that gift, and that you want another silk dress, the color of sea water, with many golden fish swimming in it. If there is in the world such a fabric, and he will give it to you as a gift, then you promise you will marry him."

The girl felt comforted, and when she went to see her father, she told him that she wanted another dress made with the fabric described by the nurse. Otherwise, she would not even dream of marrying him. To make a long story short, the king called the usual servant, and after many months of travel, Tonino came home with a dress the color of sea water and with fish swimming inside it, because he had bought it from the Jewish merchant who had sold him the first dress.

The king's daughter, when she saw that she was given this other dress as well, was silent as a statue, and was so distraught she no longer knew where she was. So, she went to her nurse and told her of her misfortune. The nurse said: "Listen, dear girl, all is not yet lost. We will try another trick and if this one doesn't work, then we will think of a different remedy. Go to the king and tell him that the dress is beautiful, but that to become his bride you need another one that is woven through with tiny golden bells and chains. If he can find such a dress in this world, then he is really very good." The girl, then, standing before the king, made her request. The king thought his daughter quite fickle, but since he was in love with her and wanted to marry her at all costs, he could not refuse her. So, the king called Tonino once again and ordered him to look for the dress made of tiny golden bells and chains and to buy it regardless of its cost. For the third time, the servant left on a journey, and after six months he brought home the very dress the king's daughter had asked for.

When the girl saw the dress with tiny golden bells and chains in her father's hands, and that he gave it to her as a gift, saying that now it was time to get married, she fainted and collapsed to the ground, as if dead. Immediately, she was carried off to her nurse's room, and when the two women were alone, the girl started rolling around the bed, tearing out her hair and crying, because she could no longer see a way of avoiding the great sin of becoming her father's wife. The nurse said: "Hey! Don't despair. I've already found a solution for you. We shall fill a bundle with your things, take a sack of money, and run away quietly, so that the king may never know where you went." The girl, who had regained some courage from that plan, said: "But how do we leave the palace without being seen by the servants, the sentinels, and all the people around?"

And the nurse replied, "You know, I have already thought of everything. We must change our appearance, with a disguise. Meanwhile, you should gather together some money and make a bundle of your things, including the three dresses the king has given you. When everything is ready, we will leave."

In secret, the girl did everything the nurse had asked her to do. And the nurse, on her part, sewed pieces of dried pumpkin onto a cambric dress, and when everything was ready, she put this dress on the king's daughter and covered her face and hands, too, so that she really looked like a large walking pumpkin. The nurse also disguised herself so that she could not be recognized. Then, in the evening, the two women left the palace and, without delay, went off into the countryside through one of the city gates, taking their chances. They walked and walked across many towns, and the people all came to see the pumpkin that was walking by itself, on its own two legs. One day, the two women finally arrived in a city where, on the stairway to the royal palace, stood the son of the king of those lands, in the company of his knights.

When the king's son saw the nurse with that woman dressed as a pumpkin, he started laughing and wanted to know who they were. He called for them, and they came into his presence. He said: "Dear nurse, where do you come from? And who is that woman? What is her name?"

The nurse answered: "Your Majesty, we come from far away and seek our fortune. This one who travels with me is called Bad Pumpkin."

The king's son exclaimed: "How funny she looks! Dear nurse, would you be willing to give me this Bad Pumpkin? I will employ her at the stables to guard the horses, and in the kitchen to work as a scullery maid. . . . Would Bad Pumpkin want to come and stay with me?"

"If that is what you wish," Bad Pumpkin answered, "I am at your service."

In short, Bad Pumpkin started working for the king's son, who commanded her to guard the horses, and wash the dishes in the kitchen. But because he thought she spoke well and found her entertaining, every day he went to converse with her. The nurse, meanwhile, had gone her separate way.

One day, the king's son said to Bad Pumpkin, who was working in the kitchen: "You know, Bad Pumpkin, every year I have this custom of giving three balls, and I invite knights and ladies from every land, even from far away."

"You are right to enjoy yourself," answered Bad Pumpkin. "You will have plenty of beautiful women to keep you happy."

The king's son said: "Bad Pumpkin, would you like to come to my ball?" And since he had in the meantime picked up a small shovel, he hit Bad Pumpkin's knees with it.

Bad Pumpkin answered: "You say this to mock me. Who am I to go to a ball?"

The night of the ball arrived, and there were very many people present, ladies and gentlemen of every rank who danced tirelessly. All of a sudden, a lady came in: she was wearing a silk dress the color of the air studded with the stars of the sky. Her face was heavenly, and her blond hair flowed down her shoulders. Everyone was enchanted by the sight of her. The king's son immediately ran toward her, took her by the arm, and started dancing with her. He was devouring her with his eyes and wanted at all costs to know her name, who she was, and where she came from. But she said nothing more to him than, "I come from Beat-the-Knees-with-a-Shovel."

The king's son had no idea what she was talking about, because he had never heard mention of a land with that ridiculous name. But to show her how happy he was about her arrival, he begged that she should accept from him, as a memento, a gold pin, which she immediately arranged in her braids. Meanwhile, midnight struck, and the king's son wanted to get something to eat. He got up from the couch and went off for a little while. But when he returned, the lady had left, and no one had noticed her leaving, so there was no way of knowing which way she had gone.

The next morning, the king's son, who because of his lovesickness did not get any sleep, went to visit Bad Pumpkin. "My dear

Bad Pumpkin, you should have seen what a beautiful lady came to my ball last night! And how well she was dressed! I have fallen in love with her, you know."

Bad Pumpkin said: "Wonderful! I am really happy for you. And who was this beautiful lady? What was her name? Where did she come from?"

The king's son exclaimed: "That is precisely my problem. She did not say anything other than that her land is called 'Beat-the-Knees-with-a-Shovel.' Then she disappeared and I have no idea where she went."

"How very strange," said Bad Pumpkin.

The king's son continued: "But tonight there is the second ball. If tonight she returns, I want to find out who this beautiful lady is. And you, Bad Pumpkin, don't you want to see my party?" And since he was holding in his hands a whip that he had picked up at the stable, he beat Bad Pumpkin's shoulders with it.

Bad Pumpkin said, "Yeah, right! You say that to mock me."

Evening came, and guests crowded the royal apartments. There was music and dancing on every corner. The king's son kept his eyes fixed on the door. All of a sudden, the lady from the previous night appeared, more splendid than before and wearing a silk dress the color of sea water, with many golden fish swimming in it. The crowd made room for her, and the king's son immediately went toward the lady, took her by the arm, and started dancing with her. And he told her he was in love with her, but that he wanted to know her name, who she was, and what land she came from. But the lady was only willing to tell him that her land was called "Beat-the-Shoulders-with-a-Whip."

The king's son said: "But dear lady, you say this to drive me to despair: I have never heard this land mentioned, nor the one you mentioned yesterday." But no matter how much he begged her, the king's son was unable to obtain any more information from her. Nevertheless, to show her how happy he was to see her there with him, as a sign of his love he took the lady's hand and placed on her finger a ring with his name engraved on the stone. Later, however, he had to leave her to give some orders, and when he returned, the lady was gone, and no one could tell him which way she had gone.

The next morning, the king's son, smitten with love, went down to see Bad Pumpkin, and said: "My dear Bad Pumpkin, the lady came last night as well! But she tricked me once again. She is surely teasing me and wants to drive me to despair. I no longer know what to do about her."

Bad Pumpkin said, "Did she really say nothing about herself?"

"Nothing! She told me that her land is called 'Beat-the-Shoulders-with-a-Whip.' Who knows what land bears this name? That's enough. Tonight, I am hosting the last ball, and I will do everything in my power to follow her when she leaves. And you, Bad Pumpkin, don't you finally want to see one of my parties?" And in saying this, he beat her feet with the tongs he had picked up while talking.

Evening came, and the crowds in the royal palace were so big that they barely fit, and everyone was dancing as happily as can be. The king's son alone was distraught, with his eyes always turned to the door so as to see whether the beautiful lady might reappear. Then, suddenly, there she was, entering the hall, and she was indescribably beautiful. She was wearing a dress woven with golden bells and chains, so that she had to move very slowly in order not to make too much noise. The crowd immediately parted to make room for her, and she walked between two rows of ladies and gentlemen. The king's son went to meet her, took her hands in his, and started dancing with her, thinking he would not leave her side all night. When it was time to rest, the king's son went to sit with this lady next to him, telling her insistently that he loved her very much and that she should do him the honor of telling him at least the name of the land that she came from.

She said: "Yes, this much I can tell you. The land I come from is called 'Beat-the-Feet-with-the-Tongs.'"

At that answer, the king's son put his head in his hands and said: "You really want to see me dead at all costs, by not telling me what I want to know." But when he lifted his head again, the lady had disappeared, and he was unable find out which way she had gone. While they were dancing, however, he had given her his portrait, in miniature, painted on a medallion to be worn around one's neck.

On that night, the king's son fell ill. He no longer ate nor slept, because he was always thinking about that lady he had fallen in love with, and did not know how to see her again or even where to go look for her. He took to his bed, and all the doctors in the kingdom were called, but they said: "There is no medicine that can heal him. This is a melancholy sickness, and there is no remedy for it."

One morning, the king's son called his mother and told her, "Mother, I have a request."

The queen said: "Speak, dear son, and I will do everything I can to make you happy, and to comfort and heal you from this illness."

He said: "I want a herb soup, and Bad Pumpkin must be the one to make it."

His mother exclaimed: "My goodness! Aren't you worried about what that scullery maid might do, given how dirty she always is from the sink and stable? She may put some filth in it."

"It does not matter, mother," he said. "If you love me, order Bad Pumpkin to make me this soup. I will eat it however she makes it."

The queen then went down to the kitchen and found Bad Pumpkin washing the dishes. She said: "Bad Pumpkin, clean yourself up a bit and make sure you make a soup that is just right for my son, and it must be made with your own hands. But make sure that you do not let any filth fall into it."

Bad Pumpkin said: "I will obey, but I will stay the way I am."

After the queen left, Bad Pumpkin wore a sparkling clean apron, locked the kitchen door, and made a herb soup. Inside it, she put the gold pin that the king's son had given her at the first ball, and then she had a servant bring the soup up to his room. The king's son started eating, and as he stirred the soup he found the gold pin, which he immediately recognized as his own. He could not help but cry out.

The queen said: "You found some filth in it. See, I told you so."

He said, "Not at all! It's just that I like this soup so much. Have Bad Pumpkin make another one just like it, since this one just increased my appetite."

To make a long story short, on that same morning Bad Pumpkin sent up to the king's son two other herb soups, and inside she put the ring and the portrait that he had given her at the balls. He jumped up, then, since he was no longer sick, and immediately went down to see Bad Pumpkin. When he was alone with her, he said: "I want to know who gave you the pin, the ring, and the portrait that were inside the soups."

Bad Pumpkin answered: "I received them as gifts from your very hands."

"What?" Then Bad Pumpkin told him her entire story, and, after throwing out that ugly dress made of dried-up pumpkin rind, she appeared to him the way she really was. You can imagine the joy and happiness of the king's son at that discovery! Without further ado, he took the girl by the hand and brought her to his mother, to whom he announced: "Here is the one who healed me, and now she must be my bride."

Preparations for the wedding were made, and kings and princes were invited from all over. The bride's father also came, but he did not recognize his daughter. When they were all sitting down to dine, the bride asked her father: "What about you? Are you alone? Don't you have children?"

"I had a daughter, but she ran away from home and I have been unable to find her," he answered.

"Poor daughter!" the girl said. "But she was right to leave you, because you wanted her to commit a grave sin, since you wanted her to become your wife."

"How do you even know these things?" the father replied.

"I know these things because I am that daughter of yours. Don't you recognize me? Look, here is my mother's ring."

The father recognized his daughter and begged for her forgiveness for his sin. Then they made peace and all got along in love and harmony, and thus the story ends.

■ Collodi (Carlo Lorenzini)

Donkey Skin

There once was a king so powerful, so beloved by his people, and so respected by his neighbors and allies that he could be said to be the happiest of all of the earth's monarchs. Among his many fortunes was also the fact that he had chosen as his wife a princess who was as beautiful as she was virtuous. And this fortunate couple lived like two peas in a pod.

Soon after their virtuous marriage, the queen gave birth to a daughter, who was endowed with every grace and loveliness, such that the royal couple did not wish for any more children. Luxury, abundance, and good taste reigned in this king's palace: the ministers were wise and capable, the courtiers virtuous and loving, the servants trustworthy and hard-working, and the stables vast and full of the most beautiful horses in the world, all of them covered with magnificent caparisons.

But the thing that most astonished the foreigners who came to visit those stables was that right in the middle of everything, in the most visible spot, a master donkey strutted around, showing off his huge, long ears. It was for a very good reason that the king had given the donkey such a special place of honor. You should know that this rare animal truly deserved everyone's respect, due to the fact that nature had formed him in such an extraordinary and singular way that every morning his litter, instead of being soiled, was covered with a profusion of beautiful gold coins, which were gathered just as soon as the donkey woke up.

But since misfortunes are roof tiles that fall on the king's head as much as on the heads of his subjects, and since there is no joy without some sadness mixed into it, it so happened that the queen was suddenly taken ill with a fierce illness against which neither science nor doctors were able to recommend any sort of remedy. Grief took over the palace.

Despite the proverb stating that "Marriage is the grave of love," the king was tender-hearted and deeply in love, and so he gave himself over to despair and made vows to all the divinities in his kingdom, offering his own life in exchange for the life of the wife he so adored. The gods and the fairies, however, were deaf to his every prayer.

Meanwhile the queen, who felt her last hour approaching, told her husband, who was consumed by weeping: "Before I die, don't be upset at me if I demand something of you: it is that, should you develop the desire to remarry, . . ."

At these words, the king cried so loudly it would have broken your heart to hear him. He took his wife's hands and bathed them in his tears, swearing that she caused him even greater pain with her talk of remarrying.

"No, no, my dear queen," he cried out, "tell me instead that I must follow you to the grave!"

"The state," the queen resumed with an unshakeable calm, which just increased the king's pain and suffering, "the state is right to expect a successor of you, and seeing that I only gave you a daughter, the people will want from you a son who resembles you. But with all the strength of my soul and for the sake of the love you have given me, I ask you not to give in to your people's insistence, except after you have found a princess more beautiful and better made than I am. Promise me this, and I will die happy."

Some believe that the queen, who had after all a certain amount of pride, wanted this promise at all costs because, sure as she was that in the world there was no other woman as beautiful as she, she could also be sure that the king would never marry again.

When the queen died, her husband became distraught and agitated. He wept like a cut vine-twig, sobbed day and night, and had no other concern than to take care of all the ceremonies and irksome duties of his widowed state.

But great suffering does not last.

Besides, the prominent figures of the state gathered together and went to the king, asking him to take another wife. The king felt this request to be harsh, and it became the reason for his renewed wailing. In addition, he invoked the promise he had made to the queen and challenged all of his counselors to find him a wife more beautiful and better made than his deceased bride—convinced as he was that this would be impossible.

The counselors, however, thought such promises childish, saying that beauty was not very important, as long as the queen was virtuous and capable of bearing children; that for the peace and safety of the state, an heir prince was needed; and that although the king's daughter certainly possessed all the skills necessary to become a great queen, she would have to take a foreigner as her husband—which meant that the foreigner would either bring her back to his own home or, if he reigned here with her, their children would not be considered the king's true descendants. Besides, since the king did not have any male children who bore his name, the neighboring kings might declare war and bring ruin to the state.

Touched by these considerations, the king gave his word that he would try to please his counselors. And from among all the marriageable princesses, he searched for the right one for him. Every day, he was shown beautiful portraits to choose from, but none of them had the graces of the deceased queen. And because of all this, he could never make up his mind.

But all of a sudden, and to his own disgrace, and even though until then he had been a man full of wisdom, he lost his mind and began to think that the princess his daughter was far more beautiful and graceful than his deceased wife. He let it be known that he had decided to marry her, because she alone could release him from the promise he had made to her mother.

At this brutal proposal, the young princess, who was a flower of virtue and modesty, almost fainted. She threw herself at the feet of the king her father and begged him with all the strength of her soul not to force her to commit such a grave crime.

But for the king, this strange idea had become an obsession, and he decided to consult an old druid, so as to appease the young princess's conscience. The druid, who was more ambitious than holy, did not mind sacrificing innocence and virtue for the glory of becoming the confidant of a great king, and found a clever way of insinuating himself into the king's mind. He so beautified the crime that the king was about to commit, that he even persuaded him that marrying his own daughter was a commendable action.

Encouraged by this wicked man, the king embraced him and then took leave of him. More stubborn than ever in his resolve, he ordered his daughter to prepare herself to obey him.

The young princess was torn apart by bitter sorrow and saw no other solution than to go to the house of her godmother, the Fairy Lilla. She left that very evening on a little buggy drawn by a large ram that knew all the roads of that land, and finally arrived at her destination.

The fairy, who loved the princess very much, told her that she had heard of her predicament, but that the princess should not worry, because nothing bad could happen to her as long as she faithfully followed her godmother's instructions.

"Dearest daughter," the fairy said, "it would be a grave mistake to marry your own father, but you can get yourself out of this situation without even contradicting him. Tell him that in order to satisfy a whim of yours, he must give you a dress the color of the air. Despite his great power he will never be able to do this."

The princess thanked her godmother profusely, and the next morning she repeated to her father, the king, what the fairy had told her to ask for, declaring that without the dress the color of the air she would never consent to marriage. The king, delighted and hopeful, gathered together his most skilled craftsmen and ordered them to make this fabric, under penalty of hanging them one by one should they not succeed. But he did not have to go that far. The following day, they brought him the dress he had requested, and when the sky is strewn with golden clouds, it does not have a color more beautiful than the color of this fabric, when it was unfolded.

Deeply afflicted, the princess did not know how to get out of this mess, for the king was pushing her to conclude their marriage. So, she went back to her godmother, who was surprised that her remedy had not worked and recommended that the princess try to ask for another dress, this time, the color of the moon.

The king could not deny his daughter anything and sent out for more capable craftsmen, ordering them to make a dress the color of the moon. He was so pressed to have it right away that in under twenty-four hours he received it, nice and ready to wear.

The princess was more infatuated at first by the magnificent dress than she was upset by her father's passionate attentions. But as soon as she got together with her ladies and her nurse, she became despondent.

The Fairy Lilla, who knew everything, came to the help of the disconsolate princess, and told her: "Either I am no longer able to get anything right, or I am right to believe that if you now asked the king your father for a dress the color of the sun, he would be at a loss to give it, because it is impossible to create such a fabric. In the worst-case scenario, we will gain some time."

The princess believed the fairy and asked her father for the dress. The king, full of love for his daughter, happily gave away all the diamonds and rubies of his crown in order to obtain a fabric matching the color of the sun. And in fact, when the fabric was put on display, all those who saw it had to close their eyes because of its great and intense light. Some even say that it was then that green glasses and smoked lenses were first invented.

You can imagine the princess's reaction to that sight. A more beautiful and artistically made thing had never been seen before. She was dazzled and confused and, with the excuse that the fabric hurt her eyes, returned to her room where the fairy was waiting, blushing with shame to the roots of her hair. And when the fairy saw the dress the color of the sun, she turned red with spite.

"Well, but this time, dear daughter," she told the princess, "we shall put your father's unworthy love to a terrible test. I will ignore the fact that he believes he already has this marriage in the bag, and I am sure he will be thrown off by the request I recommend you make of him. It is about the skin of that donkey, which he dearly loves because it generously provides for all the expenses of his court. Go and tell him that you wish for that donkey's skin."

The princess was overjoyed at the thought of finding another way out of a marriage that she detested, and she was certain that her father would never consent to sacrifice the donkey he so loved. So, she went to him and told him flat out that she wanted the skin of that beautiful animal.

Although the king was baffled by this request, he did not hesitate in doing as his daughter asked. The poor donkey was sacrificed, and his skin was politely presented to the princess, who, unable to see any other way of avoiding her misfortune, was about to lose hope and give in to despair—when suddenly the fairy appeared.

"What are you doing, dear girl?" the fairy asked, upon seeing the princess tearing out her hair and scratching her beautiful face. "This is the most fortunate time of your life. Wrap yourself in the donkey's skin, leave the palace, and walk for as long as you find earth under your feet. When we sacrifice everything in the name of virtue, the gods know how to reward us. Go. I will make sure that your dresses follow you everywhere from underground, in a crate. Here is my magic wand, which I give you as a gift: every time you need your crate, strike the ground with this wand, and the crate will appear. But hurry up and leave now: no more dawdling."

The princess embraced her godmother a thousand times, begging her to never abandon her. Then she wore the donkey's ugly skin and, after dirtying her face with soot, left that magnificent palace without anyone recognizing her.

The princess's disappearance caused a great uproar.

The king, who already had a magnificent feast prepared, was desperate and could not accept his defeat. He ordered hundreds of policemen and musketeers to go in search of his daughter, but the fairy, who protected the princess, made her invisible to everyone. And thus, her disappearance had to be accepted.

Meanwhile, the princess walked for many days and many nights. She went far, and then she went farther still, and searched everywhere for employment. But although she was given a morsel of food now and then, out of charity, no one wanted anything to do with her because she was so filthy.

She finally arrived at a beautiful city, and near its gates was a farm. The farmer happened to need a scullery maid to wash rags and clean the stables where the turkeys and pigs were housed. When the farmer saw what looked like a filthy gypsy, she asked her to come into her service. And the princess accepted very gladly, tired as she was from traveling across the land.

The princess was placed in a corner of the kitchen, and for the first few days she had to suffer the mockery of the other servants, because the donkey skin she wore made her dirty and nauseating. The other servants, however, eventually accepted her because she completed the tasks she was assigned very neatly, and the farmer took her into her good graces.

Now, the princess brought the sheep out to pasture and when they were done grazing led them back indoors. She also watched the turkeys, and she did it all so well that it was as if she had done no other work her whole life. Everything flowered and prospered in her hands.

One day, while she was sitting near a fountain of clear water, where she often went to weep over her sad destiny, she had the idea of looking at her own reflection and was frightened by that horrible donkey skin, which served as her hat and her dress.

Ashamed of looking like that, she washed her face and hands carefully. Her hands then became whiter than ivory and her beautiful complexion returned to its original freshness. The pleasure of seeing her own beauty return made her want to bathe, and so she did. Before returning to the farm, however, she had to wear her usual disgusting donkey skin once more.

Luckily, the next day was a holiday: she had all the time she needed to have her little crate appear, clean up and comb her hair well, powder her blond hair, and wear her beautiful dress the color of air. Her room was so small that the train of her dress did not even fit in it.

The beautiful princess looked at herself with admiration and great pleasure. She felt so much pleasure, in fact, that she decided that from that moment on, she would wear all of her beautiful dresses on holidays and Sundays, one at a time, if only to amuse herself a little. And she kept up this practice faithfully.

She braided flowers and diamonds in her beautiful hair with admirable ability, and often she sighed, disappointed that she had no one to see her other than her sheep and her turkeys. Indeed, the animals loved her all the same, even when they saw her covered with the horrible donkey skin that gave her that ugly nickname among the people who worked at the farm.

On a feast day, when Donkey Skin was wearing her dress the color of the sun, the king's son, on his way back from hunting, stopped to rest at the farm where she worked and that his family owned.

That prince was young, handsome, and perfectly made: he was his father's favorite, the darling of his mother the queen, and idolized by his people. The prince was offered a country snack, which he accepted. After that he started touring the courtyards and rooms.

As he wandered here and there, he entered a dark hallway, and at the end of it he saw a locked door. Curiosity made him look through the keyhole. You can imagine his surprise when he saw a princess who was so beautiful and so magnificently dressed! Because of her noble yet modest demeanor, he took her for a goddess. The rush of passion that he felt in that instant was so powerful that he would have certainly broken through the door, had he not been held back by the respect that angel of a woman inspired in him.

He quickly left that dark and dank hallway in order to seek out information about the person who lived in that tiny room. He was told she was a menial servant, called Donkey Skin because of the animal skin with which she clothed herself, and that she was so greasy and grimy that she was disgusting to even look at and nauseating to talk to, and that they had taken her in to watch the sheep and the turkeys out of pity for her unfortunate condition.

The prince, who was not really satisfied with this explanation, realized right away that those simple folks did not know anything more than what they told him, and that it was a waste of his breath to continue asking them questions. He returned to his father's palace, more madly in love than can be described, and with the image fixed in his eyes of the divine creature he had glimpsed through the keyhole. He regretted not knocking at her door, but he swore that next time he would.

Meanwhile, that very night, love caused such turmoil in his blood that he developed a very high fever, and within a few hours he was on the brink of death.

When all remedies proved useless, the queen his mother, who had no other children but this one, gave herself over to despair. She promised the doctors great rewards, but it was all in vain: they were mustering all of their skills, yet nothing seemed to heal the prince.

In the end, they guessed that this terrible illness was caused by some secret passion and told the queen as much. The queen, full of tenderness for her son, begged him to tell her the reason for his sickness, because even if it was a matter of yielding the crown to him, the king his father would give up his throne without hesitation, as long as he could see his son happy. And if he wanted a princess for a wife, they would make any sacrifice so that he could have her, even if they were at war with her father and there were righteous reasons for their enmity. But they begged him and pleaded not to let himself die, because their own lives depended on his.

The despondent queen was unable to get to the end of this moving speech without drenching the prince's face with a flood of tears.

"My Lady," the prince began, barely able to speak, "I am not such a bad son as to desire my father's crown. May God let him live one hundred more years, and may I be the most faithful and respectful of all his subjects! As for the princess you are offering me, I have not yet thought of taking a wife. But when the time comes, you can rest assured that, dutiful as I am, I will always do your will, whatever it should cost me."

"Ah, dear son," the queen started up again, "nothing will seem impossible to us as long as we may save your life. But, dearest son, save my life and the life of your father by letting us know what it is you desire, and you can be sure that you will be satisfied."

"Well then, dear lady," he said, "since you absolutely want me to tell you what I desire, I will satisfy you—especially and above all because it would be a crime to endanger the life of the two people who are dearest to me. Well, dear mother, I desire that Donkey Skin should make me a dessert, and that, when it is ready, that it should be brought to me here."

Upon hearing such a bizarre name, the queen asked who this Donkey Skin might be.

"Dear Lady," answered one of the officers who happened to have seen her, "Donkey Skin is the ugliest of all beasts, second only to the wolf. She is a piece of filth with a dark face who lives on your farm and who looks after the turkeys."

"Her appearance and position mean nothing," said the queen. "Maybe my son has eaten some of her pastries on his way back from hunting. It must be a sick man's whim, but in the end, if this Donkey Skin actually exists, let her make him a pastry right away!"

Then she sent a servant to the farm to fetch Donkey Skin, and she ordered her to make a pastry for the prince and to use all her skills.

Some writers claim that at the very moment when the prince placed his eye on the keyhole, Donkey Skin's eyes noticed it, and that, after looking out her little window and seeing this prince who was so young, so handsome, and so well shaped, she kept his image sculpted in her heart, and that in fact quite often this memory cost her some sighs of longing.

The fact is that Donkey Skin, whether she had actually seen the prince or only heard very good things about him, was very happy to have found a way of letting her identity be known. She locked herself in her room and threw aside that ugly and filthy skin, washed her face and hands thoroughly, tidied up her long hair, wore a nice top of shining silver and a skirt of the same material, and began preparing the pastry the prince was coveting. She took some fine flour, some eggs, and the freshest butter. And while she was busy kneading the dough, whether by accident or on purpose, a ring she wore on her finger fell into the dough and settled there. As soon as the pastry was cooked, she put on her horrible donkey skin and handed the pastry over to the officer and asked him for news of the prince. The officer, however, did not even bother answering and ran immediately to the prince with the pastry. The prince greedily snatched it from his hands and ate it with such voraciousness that the doctors who were in attendance immediately pronounced that this excessive hunger was not a good sign at all.

And it is true that the prince almost choked on the ring, which he found in a slice of the pastry, but he was able to deftly take it out of his own mouth, slowing down his furious eating. He examined the stunning emerald set in a gold ring, which was so narrow that he realized it could only fit the most graceful and charming finger in the world.

The prince kissed the ring a thousand times, put it into under his pillow, and every once in a while, when he believed no one was watching, took it out to look at it. It would be impossible to explain just how much he wracked his brains to figure out how he could meet the woman to whom this ring belonged. He did not dare hope that if he asked for Donkey Skin, the one who made the pastry he requested, that they would let her come to him. He did not even have the courage to tell a living soul what he saw from the keyhole, for fear that they would mock him or consider him delusional. Alas, all these thoughts tormented him so very much that he was overtaken by a great fever again, and the doctors, not knowing what to do, declared to the queen that her son was lovesick. The queen immediately went to her son along with the king, who himself was unable to find peace. "My dear son, my dear, dear son," said the grieving king, "do reveal the name of the woman you want, because we swear that we shall give her to you, even if she were the vilest of all of this earth's slaves."

The queen embraced the prince and repeated the king's promise. The prince, softened by the weeping and caresses of the authors of his days, told them: "Dear father and dear mother, I would never think of tying a knot that might hurt you, and the proof that I am speaking the truth," he added, taking the emerald out from under his pillow, "is this: that I will marry the woman whose finger shall fit this ring, whoever she might be. For it would be impossible that the one with such a graceful and tiny finger should be a peasant or a criminal."

The king and the queen took the ring into their hands, examined it with great curiosity, and ended up saying what the prince had already said—namely, that the ring would not fit anyone except a woman from a good family. The king, then, after embracing the prince and begging him to be healed, left the room and ordered that drums, flutes, and trumpets announce throughout the city, through his heralds, that anyone could simply come to the palace and try on a ring, and the one whose finger fit it perfectly would marry the heir to the throne.

First the princesses arrived, then the duchesses, the marchionesses, and the baronesses. But no matter how much they all tried to make their fingers thinner, not one of them was able to put on the ring. They even tried with the seamstresses, who may have been very pretty, but their fingers were too large. The prince was beginning to feel better, and it was he who tried to put the ring on any hopeful woman who wished for a chance. Finally, it was the waitresses' turn, and these, too, ended up like the others. Every single lady had tried in vain to wear the ring, and so the prince wanted to try it on cooks, scullery maids, and shepherdesses: all were brought before him. But their chubby, stubby fingers could not go through the ring beyond the fingernail.

"Was that Donkey Skin, who a few days ago baked me some pastry, also summoned?" asked the prince.

Everyone began laughing and answered no, because she was too filthy and disgusting.

"Fetch her right away," said the king. "Let it not be said that I made a single exception."

Laughing and joking, they went looking for the turkey keeper.

The princess, who had heard the drums and the band of the military heralds, had already imagined that her ring was the cause of all this hubbub. She loved the prince, and because true love is modest and shy, she was always afraid that some lady might have a finger as tiny as her own. So, she was filled with joy when they came seeking her out and knocking on her door.

From the very moment she heard that they were looking for a finger on which her ring would fit, a vague hope had advised her to comb her hair more expertly than usual and to wear her beautiful silver top and the skirt with lace trimmings, studded with emeralds. As soon as she heard a knock on the door and someone calling her to go to the king, she put on her donkey skin quick as a flash and opened the door. At first, the courtiers teased her and told her that the king was looking for her and wanted her to marry his son. Then, among the wildest laughter, they brought her to the prince. He too was stunned by the girl's odd clothing and could not believe that she was the same person he had seen with his own eyes, dazzling with beauty!

Sad and confused for having made this huge mistake, he asked her:

"Are you the one living in that dark hallway, in the third courtyard of the farmhouse?"

"Yes, sir," she answered.

"Show me your hand," he said, trembling and with a loud sigh.

Can you guess who was the most surprised of them all? The king and the queen, and all the chamberlains and great lords of the court, when they saw emerging from the black and grimy skin a delicate little hand, white and rosy, with the most beautiful little finger in the world onto which the ring slid effortlessly. Then, as the princess shrugged slightly, the donkey skin fell off, and she appeared in all her beauty, so dazzlingly beautiful that the prince, although he was still quite weak, fell at her feet and embraced her with such ardor that she blushed. Practically no one, however, noticed her blush, because the king and queen also came to embrace her with much tenderness and asked her whether she was happy to marry their son.

The princess, confused by so much affection and by the love shown her by this handsome prince, was about to thank them all, when the ceiling of the hall opened up and the Fairy Lilla, lowering herself inside a carriage braided with the branches and the flowers of the lilies after which she was named, told with infinite grace the princess's whole story. The king and queen were delighted to hear that Donkey Skin was a great princess and redoubled their attentions. The prince became ever more sensitive to the princess's virtues, and his love grew because of all the wonderful things he heard about her. His impatience to marry the princess was so strong that it did not even leave him time to prepare their majestic wedding in an appropriate manner.

The king and queen, enamored of their new daughter-in-law, caressed her a thousand times and always kept her in their arms. Since she had stated that she would not be able to marry the prince without the consent of the king her father, they invited him to the wedding, but without disclosing the bride's identity. The Fairy Lilla, who was naturally the one in charge of everything, decided it should be so, in order to prevent anything bad from happening.

Princes and kings arrived from every land—some in litters, some in carriages. The ones from farthest away came riding elephants, tigers, and eagles. The most magnificent and most powerful of them all, however, was the princess's father, who, fortunately, had forgotten his strange, twisted form of love and had married a beautiful, widowed queen.

When the princess went to meet him, he recognized her immediately and embraced her with great tenderness, before she even had time to throw herself at his feet. The king and queen introduced their son to him, and the princess's father was wonderfully courteous to his future son-in-law. The wedding was celebrated with a lavishness so great that it cannot be described in words. The young couple, who cared little for such magnificence, only had eyes and thoughts for each other.

The prince's father had his son crowned on the same day and, kissing his hand, placed him on the throne. After an initial resistance, his loving son eventually obeyed. The celebrations for this illustrious wedding lasted over three months, but the young couple's love would still last to this day still, given how much they cared for each other, were it not that they died one hundred years later.

It is hard to believe Donkey Skin's story to be true. But as long as there are grandmothers, mothers, and children in this world, everyone will remember it with pleasure.

- Yorick (Pietro Coccoluto Ferrigni)

The Fairies

Once upon a time, there was a widow who had two daughters. The oldest resembled her mother in every way, physically and otherwise, and everyone who met her saw the very image of her mother. Mother and daughter were both very unpleasant and so puffed up with pride that no one ever wanted to go near them. Living with them was downright impossible. The younger daughter, on the contrary, was the spitting image of her father. She had a sweet demeanor and a good heart, and she was beautiful—so very beautiful, in fact, that nowhere could one possibly find another quite so beautiful. And, of course, because like attracts like, the mother was crazy about the older daughter, Cecchina, and felt a strong aversion bordering on repugnance for the other. She made her younger daughter eat in the kitchen and do all the chores and housework.

Among her other obligations, the poor girl had to go fetch water at a fountain that was over a mile and a half away. She had to do this twice a day and bring back a full pitcher of water each time.

One day, just as she arrived at the fountain, a poor old woman appeared next to her and begged her for something to drink.

"But of course, sweet grandmother," answered the beautiful girl. "Wait, let me rinse out the pitcher first."

And she immediately gave the jug a good rinse, filled it with fresh water, and offered it to the old woman by holding it up with both of her hands, so that she could drink more easily. After she finished drinking, the little grandmother said: "You are as beautiful as you are kind and well-mannered, my child, and I want to leave you with a gift."

As it turned out, the poor old woman was actually a fairy, who had disguised herself to test the girl's kindness. The fairy continued: "My gift to you is that, with every word you utter, a flower or a precious stone will come out of your mouth."

The girl arrived at her house with a full pitcher. She was a few minutes late, and her mother scolded her harshly for that small delay.

"Mother, please be patient, I apologize," said the daughter, humbly, and as she spoke, two roses, two pearls, and two large diamonds came out of her mouth.

"But what is this?! . . . ," the mother exclaimed, stunned. "Am I mistaken or are you spitting pearls and diamonds?! . . . How come, my child?"

It was the first time in her entire life that she had called her "my child," or spoken to her affectionately. The girl naïvely explained what had happened to her at the fountain, and during her story, you can imagine the rubies and topazes that spilled out of her mouth!

"Well, what good luck!" exclaimed her mother. "I must immediately send my other daughter, too. Listen, Cecchina, look at what comes out of your sister's mouth when she speaks. Would you like to have the same gift yourself? All you have to do is go to the fountain, and if an old woman asks you for a drink, you must be kind and give it to her."

"Yeah, right, as if I had nothing better to do!" answered that rude girl. "You want me to go to the fountain? At this late hour?!"

"I am telling you to go. Right now!" her mother yelled.

The girl started mumbling, but even as she mumbled she went on her way, carrying in her arms the most beautiful silver jug in the house. You can picture her pride, of course, and her laziness. As soon as she arrived at the fountain, a magnificently dressed lady appeared, and asked the girl for a sip of water. It was the same fairy that had appeared earlier to the other sister, but she had taken on the looks and clothing of a princess, to see the full extent of this girl's bad manners.

"What do you think?" replied the proud girl, "That I came all the way here just to give you a drink?! . . . Sure! . . . I came just to quench your ladyship's thirst, nothing else! . . . Look, if you are thirsty, the fountain is right there."

"You have bad manners, my girl," the fairy answered without getting angry in the least, "and since you are so rude, I shall give you this gift: that with every word you utter, a toad or a snake shall fall out of your mouth."

As soon as the mother saw her daughter return from a distance, she cried with great joy, "So, Cecchina, how did it go?"

"Don't bother me, mom!" replied the brat. And as she spoke, she spit out two vipers and two warty toads.

"Dear God! . . . What do I see?" exclaimed her mother. "This must be entirely your sister's fault. But she will pay for what she's done!" And she went to hit her other daughter, but the poor girl ran away in haste and took refuge in the nearby forest.

The king's son was on his way back from hunting and ran into her on a footpath. Seeing she was so beautiful, he asked what she was doing in that place all alone, and why she was crying so much.

"My mother," she said, "kicked me out of the house and wanted to hit me."

The king's son, who saw five or six pearls and as many diamonds come out of that cute little mouth as the girl spoke, begged her to tell him how such a marvel was possible. And the girl told him in great detail all that happened to her.

The royal prince fell in love with her instantly. And considering that the fairy's gift was worth much more than any great dowry another bride might bring, he took her without delay to his father the king's palace and married her.

The other sister in the meantime became so hated by everyone that her own mother kicked her out of the house. And after running off in vain looking for someone who would take her in, the wretched girl went to die at the edge of the woods.

MORAL

Emeralds, pearls, and diamonds
Dazzle the eye with their bright splendor.
But sweet words and sweet tears
Often have greater power and value.

ANOTHER MORAL

The kindness that kindles all beautiful souls
Sometimes costs bitter grief and pain.
But sooner or later virtue shines,
And when one least expects it, obtains its prize.

Sunbeam

Once upon a time, there was a woman who was a baker and had a daughter as dark as charcoal and uglier than mortal sin. Mother and daughter survived by baking other people's bread, and Little Charcoal—as everyone called the daughter—worked from morning to night. "Hey, heat up the water!" "Hey, keep kneading!" Then, with a wooden tray under her arm and a cloth folded into a doughnut on top of her head, Little Charcoal went all over town to pick up loaves and rolls to bake. Later, with a basket slung over her shoulders, again she went all over town to deliver the baked loaves and rolls. In short, she did not have a moment's rest.

Little Charcoal was always in a good mood. She looked like a pile of soot: her hair was ruffled, her feet bare and caked with mud, and she wore nothing but rags. Still, her laughter rang from one end of the road to the other.

"Little Charcoal sounds like a hen clucking," the neighbors said.

Shortly after sunset, the two bakers locked themselves inside the house and did not show even the tip of their nose. During the winter, this behavior was understandable. But in summer, when the entire neighborhood enjoyed the cool air and the moonlight, it made no sense. Were they crazy, mother and daughter, to stay locked inside the house with all that heat? The neighbors racked their brains to figure out what those two were up to.

"Dear bakers, come out in the cool air, come out!"

"We are cooler in the house."

"Dear bakers, look at that beautiful moonlight, look!"

"There is better light in the house."

Well, this made no sense! The neighbors began to spy and eavesdrop at the two women's doorstep. From the cracks they saw a dazzling light, and once in a while they heard the mother saying, "Sunbeam, my dear Sunbeam, you will be queen if God wills it!"

And Little Charcoal sounded like a hen clucking.

The neighbors were right when they said that the two had gone mad!

Every night was like this, until midnight: "Sunbeam, my dear Sunbeam, you will be queen if God wills it!"

When the story reached the king's ear, he became furious and demanded that the bakers be brought to him.

"Old witch, if you keep this up, I will have you thrown to the bottom of a dungeon, you and your Little Charcoal!"

"Your majesty, none of it is true. The neighbors are liars."

Little Charcoal laughed even in front of the king.

"Ah! Why are you laughing?"

And he threw the mother and daughter in jail.

But at night, from the cracks of the cell door, the jailor saw a great splendor in that ugly room. It was a dazzling splendor, and, once in a while, he heard the older woman saying, "Sunbeam, my dear Sunbeam, you will be queen if God wills it!"

And Little Charcoal sounded like a hen clucking. Her laughter rang throughout the prison. The jailor went to the king and told him everything. After that, the king became even more furious than he already was.

"So, is this how they are taking it? Let them be placed in the jail for criminals, then, in the underground dungeon."

It was a horrible room with neither air nor light, and humidity seeped into its every corner: it was definitely not a livable place. But at night, even in the underground jail for criminals, there was a dazzling splendor, and the older woman could be heard saying, "Sunbeam, my dear Sunbeam, you will be queen if God wills it!"

The jailor went back to the king and reported everything. The king, this time, was quite surprised. He gathered the Royal Council. But while some of the counselors wanted the bakers' heads chopped off, the others thought the two women were insane and should be set free.

"After all, what is that woman saying? *If God wills it.* What was the harm in that? If God willed it, not even His Majesty would be able to prevent it."

"Right! That is indeed true."

The king ordered the women to be set free. The bakers went back to their work. There were no others who could compete with their baking skills, and their old customers immediately came back to them. Even the queen wanted her bread baked by them. Therefore, Little Charcoal, her feet bare and caked with mud, often went up the stairs of the royal palace. The queen would ask her, "Little Charcoal, why don't you wash your face?"

"Your Majesty, I have fine skin and water would ruin it."

"Little Charcoal, why don't you comb your hair?"

"Your Majesty, I have fine hair and the comb would pull it out."

"Little Charcoal, why don't you buy yourself a pair of shoes?"

"Your Majesty, I have delicate feet and shoes would give me calluses."

"Little Charcoal, why does your mother call you *Sunbeam?*"

"I will be queen, if God wills it!"

The queen had fun with this, and Little Charcoal laughed and laughed, carrying a baker's tray on her head with the loaves and rolls of the royal household. The neighbors who heard her go by would say, "Little Charcoal sounds like a hen clucking!"

Meanwhile, every night the same thing happened. The neighbors were eaten up with curiosity. And as soon as they saw that dazzling splendor and heard the older woman's refrain, off they went, all at the bakers' door. They couldn't help but make things up.

"Bakers, please be so kind as to lend me your sieve. Mine is torn."

Little Charcoal opened the door and handed over the sieve.

"What? You are in the dark? While I was knocking, I saw light."

"Well, you must have been mistaken."

"Bakers, please, lend me a needle. Mine are all broken, and I need to finish a sewing job."

Little Charcoal opened the door and handed over the needle.

"What? You are in the dark? When I was knocking, I saw light."

"Well, you must have been mistaken."

Eventually, these things reached the prince's ear. He was already sixteen and very haughty. Whenever he saw Little Charcoal on the stairs, with a tray on her head or a basket on her shoulders, he turned the other way so as not to look at her. She disgusted him. And once he even spit on her. On that occasion, Little Charcoal went home crying.

"What happened, dear daughter?"

"The prince spit on me."

"God's will be done. The prince is master."

The neighbors gloated, "The prince spit on her. Serves *Sunbeam* right!"

Another day, the prince met Little Charcoal on the landing. He thought she had bumped into him slightly with her tray, and, since he was vexed, he kicked her in the stomach. Little Charcoal fell down the stairs. Her loaves and rolls were all dusty and misshapen now. Who would have the courage to bring them back to the queen? Little Charcoal went home crying and sad.

"What happened, dear daughter?"

"The prince kicked me in the stomach and made me drop everything."

"God's will be done! The prince is master."

The neighbors were so delighted they were bursting out of their own skin.

"The prince kicked *Sunbeam* in the stomach! Serves her right!"

A few years later, the prince decided to take a wife and sent for the daughter of the King of Spain. But his ambassador arrived too late: the daughter of the King of Spain had gotten married the previous day. The prince wanted the ambassador hung. But the ambassador quickly showed him that he had reached his destination half a day more quickly than anyone else. So, the prince sent him for the daughter of the King of France. But the ambassador arrived too late: the daughter of the King of France had gotten married the day before. The prince wanted at all costs to hang that traitorous ambassador who never arrived in time, but the ambassador, in the blink of an eye, proved to him that it had taken him a half a day less than anyone else to travel to his destination. So, the prince sent him to the Great Turk to ask for his daughter. But the ambassador arrived too late once again: the Great Turk's daughter had gotten married the day before. The prince could not accept any of this and started crying. The king, the queen, and all the ministers surrounded him.

"Were there not any princesses left? There was the daughter of the King of England. Let her be sent for."

The poor ambassador left in a flash, walking day and night until he arrived in England. But it was the will of fate! The daughter of the King of England had also gotten married the day before.

You can imagine the prince's frustration!

One day, to distract himself, the prince went hunting. He got lost in the woods, far from his companions, and wandered all day, unable to find his way home. Finally, in the evening, he arrived at a farmhouse among the trees. Through the open door, he saw an old man inside. He had a great white beard and was preparing his dinner by a fire.

"Good man, could you show me the way out of the woods?"

"Ah, finally you have arrived!"

As soon as he heard that thunderous voice, the prince felt his skin crawl.

"Good man, I do not know you. I am the prince."

"Prince or no prince, take that hatchet and chop me some wood."

Afraid of what might happen, the prince chopped him some wood.

"Prince or no prince, go fetch me some water at the fountain."

Afraid of what might happen, the prince took the jar in his arms and went to the fountain.

"Prince or no prince, serve me at table."

And afraid of what might happen, the prince served him at table. When the old man had finished eating, he gave the prince his leftovers.

"You may rest over there: that is your place."

The poor prince curled up on a bit of straw in a corner but was unable to sleep. That old man was the wizard, the master of the woods. Whenever he left his home, he laid an enchanted net around it, and thus the prince could not escape. He was the wizard's prisoner and slave.

Meanwhile, the king and queen grieved their son's death and wore mourning clothes. But one day, mysteriously, the news reached them that the prince was the wizard's prisoner and slave. The king immediately sent off his couriers to find his son.

"The wizard will receive all the riches of the kingdom, if only he releases the king's son!"

"I am richer than he is."

At the wizard's answer, the king's consternation was great. He sent his couriers out again.

"What did he want? Just say the word. The king would give even the blood in his veins."

"I want one loaf and one roll sieved, kneaded, and baked by the queen's hand, and the prince will be free."

"Oh, this was nothing!"

The queen sieved the flour, kneaded it, made a loaf and a roll, heated up the oven with her own hands, and baked the bread. But she did not know how to do any of this: the loaf and the roll came out burned and hard as rocks.

When the wizard saw them, he curled up his nose.

"Those are good for the dogs!"

And he tossed them to his mastiff.

The queen again sieved the flour, kneaded it, and made another loaf and another roll. She then heated the oven with her own hands and baked them. But she did not know how to do any of that. The loaf and the roll came out raw. When the wizard saw them, he curled up his nose.

"Those are good for the dogs!"

And he tossed them to his mastiff.

The queen tried, and tried again, but her bread always came out either too cooked or too raw—and meanwhile the poor prince was still the wizard's prisoner and slave.

The king summoned the Royal Council.

"Your Holy Majesty," said one of his ministers, "let's see whether the wizard is a soothsayer. The queen will sieve the flour, knead the dough, shape the loaf and the roll, and then to heat the oven and bake the bread, we shall call Little Charcoal!"

"Good! Very good!"

And so, they did. But the wizard curled his nose.

"Loaf and roll, wash your face!"

And he tossed them to the dog. He knew that Little Charcoal had been involved.

"Then," said the minister, "there is only one remedy."

"What?" asked the king.

"Have the prince marry Little Charcoal. This way the wizard will have his bread sieved, kneaded, and baked by the hands of the queen, and the prince will be freed."

"It truly is God's will!" said the king. "Sunbeam, Sunbeam, you will be queen if God wills it."

And he pronounced a royal decree declaring the prince and Little Charcoal to be husband and wife. The wizard had his loaf and roll sieved, kneaded, and baked to perfection by the hands of the queen, and the prince was finally set free.

Let us now turn to the prince, who wanted nothing to do with Little Charcoal.

"That pile of soot for a wife? That ugly baker, a queen?"

"But there was a royal decree!"

"Really? The king declared it, and he can undeclare it."

Little Charcoal was now a queen and had gone to live in the royal palace. But she did not want to wash, or comb her hair, or change her clothes, or wear shoes.

"When the prince arrives, then I will clean up."

The prince arrived.

"When it's time to go to bed, then I will clean up."

Was that possible? And locked in her room, Little Charcoal waited for the prince to visit her. But there was no convincing him to do so.

"That baker disgusts me! Better to be dead than to be married to her!"

Little Charcoal heard these words and started laughing.

"He will come, rest assured. He will come."

"I will come? Watch me!"

The prince, who had lost his mind and held a saber in his fist, ran to Little Charcoal's room: he wanted to chop off her head. The door was closed. The prince looked through the keyhole, and the saber fell from his hand. Inside, he saw a beauty never seen before, a true *sunbeam*.

"Open up, dear princess! Open up!"

And Little Charcoal, from inside, teased him.

"Pile of soot!"

"Open up! You are the princess of my soul!"

And Little Charcoal, laughing:

"Ugly baker!"

"Open up, dear Little Charcoal!"

Then the door opened, and the young couple embraced.

That evening, the wedding was celebrated, and the prince and Little Charcoal lived a long and happy life.

But the rest of us stay here, instead, and grind our teeth.

Golden Feather

Once upon a time there were a king and a queen who had a daughter as beautiful as the moon and the sun. She was so vivacious, however, that the noise she made turned the entire royal castle upside down. She was as impish and mischievous as only a little girl who was never reprimanded by her parents could be. The bigger her tantrums, the more her parents laughed.

"Ha ha, she's so vivacious! Ha ha, she's so vivacious!"

But one day, they came to regret their excessive indulgence. The king was about to go hunting when he found a little old lady at the door of the palace. She was in rags, bent over, and leaned on a cane to hold herself up.

"What do you want, good woman?"

"I am looking for the king."

"I am the king."

The old lady bowed to him and gave him a letter.

"It's from the King of Spain."

The King of Spain requested lodging in the royal palace for the old woman for just one night and asked that she be treated as if he were there himself.

"Don't ask her where she comes from, nor where she is going. You will not regret being kind to her."

The king thought it a joke and gave orders that a tiny room be prepared in the attic, and that the old woman eat with the servants.

"Thank you, Your Majesty," the old woman said.

And she went to curl up in the attic.

She ate quietly in a corner with the servants, when suddenly the little sprightly princess came to their table and dumped the salt and pepper shakers into the old woman's soup.

"You will be amazed by the taste!"

And all the servants burst out laughing.

"Ha ha, she's so vivacious! Ha ha, she's so vivacious!"

The old woman did not say a thing and ate her soup as if nothing happened.

When they found out what their daughter had done, the king and queen also burst out laughing.

"Ha ha, she's so vivacious! Ha ha, she's so vivacious!"

After getting up from the table the old woman looked for her stick but could not find it. She searched in the fireplace and saw that the stick was already half burnt off by the fire while the princess, bent over laughing, said to her, "It's nice and hot—it will work better!"

And all the servants laughed.

"Ha ha, she's so vivacious! Ha ha, she's so vivacious!"

The old woman took the stick out of the fire and left the kitchen leaning on it, as if nothing happened. The king and queen burst out laughing, too, when they found out.

The next morning, on her way out, the old woman found the princess waiting for her on the landing.

> Old woman, where do you come from and
> where are you going?
> Old woman, what souvenir will you leave me?

And the old woman answered, grumbling:

> Where I'm going and where I come from
> The rain falls and the wind blows.
> With the wind you shall arrive and
> With the rain you shall then leave.

The old woman touched the princess with her stick, went down the stairs, and disappeared.

From that day on, the princess began to lose weight. She did not become thinner, nor did she become ugly—in fact, she grew normally, but from one month to the next she felt herself become lighter and lighter. When she reached the age of eighteen, she had turned into a beautiful young woman with a white complexion and a mane of golden hair, but she weighed less than a feather, and the lightest breath could carry her away.

You can imagine the despair of the king and queen. They had to keep all the windows in the royal palace shut. They could not take their daughter outside for fear that the wind might carry her off to who knows where. The princess quickly grew bored with being shut inside like this, but the king and queen did not want anyone to know about their daughter's misfortune. So, in order to distract her, they spent their days blowing her around and making her fly down the corridors and through the halls of the palace.

The princess found it enormously amusing to feel herself float around in the air, and called out, "Blow, Your Majesty! More, Your Majesty!"

The king and queen were breathless and panting from making her fly higher and higher. But the higher she rose, the louder she screamed, "Blow, Your Majesty! More, Your Majesty!"

The king and queen could hardly spend their entire day blowing their daughter around, but when they stopped, the princess would pout and cry. And seeing her so sad, the poor parents would immediately go back to blowing, the king from one side and the queen from the other, and the princess clapped her hands and cheered up very quickly.

"Blow, Your Majesty! More, Your Majesty!"

They propelled her all the way up to the ceiling, and they ran after her in the corridors, blowing, blowing, and blowing some more just to keep her happy, because their poor daughter could not enjoy any other distraction. And when they rested, out of breath from blowing so much, the king and queen complained, "Unfortunate daughter, who cast this spell on you?"

One day, as she heard these words, the princess remembered the old woman's answer, and said, "It was that old woman!"

"How did it happen?"

"She answered me,

Where I'm going and where I come from
The rain falls and the wind blows.
With the wind you shall arrive and
With the rain you shall then leave.

If he could find the old woman, the king would give her any treasure just to undo the spell. But who knew upon what land that witch's eyes were shining?

So, the king and queen continued to blow and push Golden Feather up high—for that is what they now called their daughter, since she was blonde and her hair looked like spun sugar. Golden Feather's only thought was to have fun that way. She ate with gusto, grew in size, became even more beautiful than she already was. However, her weight had decreased so very much that an actual feather seemed made of lead by comparison. A small breath was enough to make her rise high, but that was never enough for her, unless the king and queen blew hard.

"Blow, Your Majesty! More, Your Majesty!"

The king and queen could not stand it any longer. After two years of entertaining their daughter like this, they realized that their faces were becoming long and muzzle-shaped from all that blowing. And in the meantime, Golden Feather had become more demanding, always wanting to be blown around in the air. It's true that she had no other distraction, but could her parents be expected to spend their entire life blowing? And once they died, who would have the patience to continue? The king and queen could not find peace.

Meanwhile, the fame of the princess's beauty had spread across the world, and the King of Portugal sent for her as a bride for his prince, who was ready to marry.

Great embarrassment ensued. If Golden Feather's parents were to answer no, the King of Portugal might take offense and declare war. Consequently, the king and queen spent an entire day and a whole night discussing matters. In the end, they decided to take a year's time to conclude the wedding.

The worst was when the prince wrote that he intended to come and visit his betrothed so as to meet her in person. The king and queen were disturbed at the thought of having to disclose the princess's troubling situation.

Seeing them so afflicted that they no longer had the will and the strength to blow and make her fly up in the air, the princess said: "Your Majesty, since the old woman grumbled, *With the wind you shall come*, let me go, for my destiny wills it."

There were tears and desperate cries.

"Never, dear daughter! Never!"

But the princess was stubborn and said: "Let me go. My heart tells me that good things will come of it."

The king and queen finally agreed. And one day, while a furious mistral wind was blowing, they brought their daughter on a stretcher to the top of a mountain. They hugged her, blessed her, and abandoned her to the mercy of the wind. In a flash, she was lifted up and pushed so high that, within minutes, the king and queen lost sight of her.

Now let us leave these two to their tears and follow the princess instead.

She was afflicted, too, but after a few hours of travel, she was transported to great heights with a speed that she had never experienced before, and she calmed down and started looking below and around herself. What a view! Cities, mountains, plains, rivers, forests, everything was flowing underneath her, as if she were the one who was still and everything else instead were swiftly flying in the opposite direction. When the wind occasionally blew less powerfully, she descended a bit, spinning in the air, only to be lifted up again and tossed all the way into the clouds, always moving forward, passing new cities, new mountains, new plains, thicker forests, and wider rivers. Suddenly, she realized that the earth had vanished. Water, water, and more water: she could see nothing but water moving into foaming waves, and then water and more water. . . . It was the sea.

When the wind let her descend, Golden Feather was afraid. One time the spray of the waves reached her face, and she thought herself lost. But then a gust of wind lifted her up again, pushing her back to her speedy flight. . . . And she saw more water, always more and more water!

Then, it was as if the sun was smothered by the sea, and the stars began glimmering high in the dark sky. Her heart grew smaller and smaller, and she started weeping and crying, "Oh, mommy! Oh, mommy!"

The wind, however, rocked her so sweetly that her eyes grew heavier and heavier. Without even realizing it, she fell asleep, just as if she were in her own bed.

How many miles did she travel in her sleep? Who could possibly know?

At dawn, when she opened her eyes, she felt her chest releasing, and saw the verdant plains below her once again. Golden Feather was flying so low that she could easily make out country houses, trees, streets, streams, and people. Human beings were the size of ants! And descending even further, she realized that the peasants were watching her, lifting up their arms to point her out to others. She even heard their voices saying, "What could that be? Is it a bird of ill omen?"

The sun was high already. The wind had calmed and seemed to really enjoy rocking the princess in the air.

Her hair had come undone and flew around her neck, her clothes puffed up and flapped about like wings holding her up. Was she finally about to arrive where her destiny, good or bad, wanted to take her?

Meanwhile, her stomach began to grumble. For a full day and a whole night, she had not swallowed anything, not even a drop of water. How was she supposed to find food up there in the air?

A flock of birds flew by.

"Little birds, little birds, give me something of what you have in your beak. I am dying of hunger."

"Our babies are waiting for us in their nests: this food is for them."

The birds went on their way. The wind pushed her higher. A row of clouds went by.

"Clouds, beautiful clouds, give me a drop of your water. I am dying of thirst."

"This water is for the fields. We are in a hurry."

Around sunset, she saw a rocky mountain in the distance, and on top of the mountain a palace as big as a city, which seemed made of white and black marble, marvelous to behold. Golden Feather gathered some courage and thought:

"If only I could stop there! Dear mother, I feel like I am dying!"

She did in fact faint from weakness and no longer saw or heard anything. And when she finally woke up, she found herself lying on the balcony of the very palace she had seen from afar.

She went down the stairway that led inside, hoping to run into someone, but there was not a single living soul. The walls of the room were made of white marble, and the moldings, the frames of the doors, and the columns were all made of gray marble. Tables, chairs, beds, furniture, all of it was made of white or gray marble. And there was a strange smell of salt and pepper everywhere.

She opened a cupboard and saw platters holding a variety of prepared foods, as well as sandwiches, fruit, and sweets. Everything, however, was carved in white or gray marble and had a smell so strong that it made her sneeze. Pushed by hunger, she brought one of those fake foods to her lips. She was surprised because they were actually made of salt and pepper. Then she realized that the entire palace was built with smooth boulders of salt and pepper so firmly kneaded together that they looked just like marble.

She remembered the salt and pepper shakers she had spilled into the old woman's soup when she was a child and said to herself: "This is her palace. This is how she is punishing me."

And as she wept, she cried out: "Old lady, oh old lady! Give me something to eat, old lady!"

A very soft voice answered her from afar: "There is so much stuff around! Taste it and you will learn just how delicious it is!"

Golden Feather had no choice. So, she took a sandwich and an apple and started nibbling on them. They actually tasted like bread and like apple, but salted and peppered!

And Golden Feather wept again and cried out: "Old lady, old lady! Give me something to drink, old lady!"

The soft voice answered her from afar: "There is so much stuff around! Taste it and you will learn just how delicious it is!"

She took a bottle and a cup, but the water she poured was murky. Still, because she had no choice, Golden Feather drank it all in one gulp. Dear God! Even the water was salted and peppered. And this is what happened every day, and she never saw another human face in that huge palace. Even the trees in the garden and the flowers and the herbs were made of salt and pepper. Golden Feather kept sneezing, with big tear drops running down her cheeks.

Let's go back now to the Prince of Portugal, who had gone to visit the princess. Weeping copiously, the king and queen told him, "The princess has been carried off by the wind!"

At first, the prince thought they were mocking him. But then, after he heard Golden Feather's story, he said, "I am going to look for her."

"Where in the world will you go?"

"I will go to the end of the world if I have to. I want to find her at all costs."

He climbed on his horse and away he rode, all alone, asking everywhere he went: "Please be kind and tell me whether you have seen a beautiful girl blown by the wind through the air?"

Many took him for mad and did not even answer his question.

"Please tell me whether you have seen a beautiful girl blown by the wind through the air?"

"We saw her. She was flying across the sky. She looked like a bird of ill omen."

"And in which direction was she going?"

"Straight ahead, way up ahead."

The prince spurred on his horse. He met more people.

"Please tell me whether you have seen a beautiful girl blown by the wind through the air?"

"We saw her. She was flying across the sky. She looked like a bird of ill omen. Then the wind lifted her up, and she disappeared among the clouds."

At this news, the prince lost heart. He was about to turn back when he saw an old man among the bushes. He had a white beard that fell all the way down to his knees and held a shovel in his hands.

"Handsome knight, what are you looking for in these parts?"

"I'm searching for Princess Golden Feather, who was taken away by the wind. Please tell me whether you have seen her pass by?"

"She was asking the birds for food and the clouds for water, but the clouds and the birds did not give her anything and went on their way. Those who go, arrive. Those who seek, find. Be brave, handsome knight!"

"And who are you?"

"I am a poor old man. I am digging up a root right here, but I don't have the strength to actually do it."

"Give me your shovel, and I'll dig it up for you."

The prince got off his horse and started digging.

He dug and dug but the root would not come out.

"Be brave, handsome knight! Those who seek, find."

But no matter what the old man said, the root would not come out. Sweat dripped down his brow, and he felt that his arms were about to break.

"Be brave, handsome knight! Those who seek, find. . . . Thank you! Here it is!"

And the old man stretched out his hand toward the dirt-covered root.

"I am giving you this whistle," he said to the prince. "If you need anything, blow on it and you shall see. Take care not to lose it, though. You will not find another one like it among all the treasures of the world."

The prince thanked him, put the whistle in his pocket, climbed back on his horse, and continued on his way. He was thinking of the princess.

"If only I knew who could help me find her!"

Then he took the whistle out of his pocket and, without really believing anything would happen, cried out, "Eagle, O messenger eagle, I bid you to obey me!"

He whistled, and in no time the eagle came flying down from above, its great wings spread out.

"Messenger eagle, fly around and bring me news of my princess. I will wait for you here."

The eagle left immediately, and for two days it did not return. But on the third day, the eagle reappeared with a letter in its beak. The princess had written: "I am held prisoner in the salt-and-pepper palace of a fairy, where no living soul may enter."

Then the prince remembered the words of the old woman:

> With the wind you shall arrive and
> With the rain you shall then leave.

"All right," he thought.

He took the whistle out of his pocket and said, "Clouds, clouds, I bid you to obey me!"

He whistled, and mountains of clouds arrived from every corner of the sky, solicitous and full of rain.

"Eagle, O messenger eagle, I bid you to obey me!"

As soon as he whistled, the eagle also appeared. It swooped down and landed at his feet.

"Come on, dear eagle! Bring me to the fairy's palace of salt and pepper. And you, clouds, come behind me!"

He climbed onto the eagle, as if it were a horse. And after spreading its wings, the eagle carried him up high, away through the sky. Right behind them were clouds heavy with rain: they looked like huge mountains that darkened the sun. And away the eagle and the prince went!

When the fairy saw that storm approaching from the balcony of her palace, she realized the danger she was in. So, she immediately unleashed the southwest wind that she kept locked up in a room.

The wind met the eagle and the clouds halfway, and with its great huffing did not let them advance. The fight lasted for over two hours, and the eagle and the clouds were unable to move a single inch forward. The wind, instead of getting tired of blowing, seemed to actually gain strength from it.

"Wait a minute," said the prince.

He took the whistle out of his pocket.

"North wind, north wind, do as I ask!"

He whistled, and immediately a furious north wind rose, blowing from behind and violently pushing the eagle and the clouds forward. Within a few moments, they arrived at the fairy's palace of salt and pepper and stopped.

"Wind, I order you to calm down. Clouds, I order you to dissolve into rain!"

The prince started whistling again. It looked as if the cataracts of the sky had suddenly opened, and as the rain came down in torrents, the salt-and-pepper palace dissolved. Murky rivers of dissolved salt and pepper rushed down the mountain gorges, hurrying toward the sea.

It rained like this for seven days and seven nights, until nothing was left of the fairy's palace. The fairy also disappeared, right after repeating this phrase to the princess, who was clutching a boulder for dear life:

> *With the wind you shall arrive and*
> *With the rain you shall then leave.*

The prince climbed onto the eagle, intending to bring Golden Feather away with him. But there was no way! By eating so much salt and pepper the princess had gained back her normal weight, and the eagle could not possibly carry them both.

"Thank you, strong eagle."

The prince climbed off the eagle and set the bird free.

The princess was so happy she could not utter a single word. The prince, meanwhile, took the whistle out of his pocket and said, "Horses, O harnessed horses, do as I ask!"

He blew the whistle, and two magnificent harnessed horses emerged from underground right in front of them, chomping at the bit. He was about to put the whistle back in his pocket, when suddenly the little old man appeared, with his white beard that went all the way down to his knees—the same old man who had given the prince that gift.

"Prince, you no longer need the whistle. Return it to me, and may God accompany you home.

The prince really wanted to keep the whistle because it had been so useful!

"Try it," added the old man, "and you will see that in your hands it no longer works."

Indeed, the whistle no longer worked, and so the prince returned it to the old man.

"Thanks again, good old man."

After one month of traveling, the prince and the princess arrived safe and sound at the royal palace.

They were married amid great celebrations, and they lived happily thereafter. The princess, however, never forgot her evil deeds from when she was a child, and she made a vow never to eat either salt or pepper again for the rest of her life.

And thus ends the story of Golden Feather.

■ Gabriele D'Annunzio

The Doves (Land of Abruzzi—S. Eusanio del Sangro)

A sailor had many boats, but he never caught any fish. One day, he told his wife: "If tomorrow I don't catch any fish, I will drown myself!"

The next day, at dawn, he prepared his best pair of fishing boats, and set off to sea. The sea was calm and clear. In the distance, the man cast his nets and struggled to pull them out. However, there was only one fish in the nets, and this fish began to speak with a sweet voice while bouncing inside the net. "Don't eat me! Just one fish won't help you much!" the fish cried. "Toss me back in the water, and I'll make you rich."

As soon as he heard those words, the sailor was stupefied, and without answering, took the fish and tossed it back into the sea.

That night, he went home and told his wife, "You know what happened to me?" And he told her what had happened.

"Praise be to God!" his wife exclaimed. "Let's see what this fish will do. Tomorrow, go back to sea. Praise be to God!"

The next day, there were many fishermen on the sea, and they were all working under the sun. All their nets were coming up from the water empty. But the lucky sailor was catching fish in large numbers and with no effort.

Upon his return, his wife said, "See? Perhaps tomorrow will also be like this."

And so it was. Little by little, the sailor accumulated great wealth. He bought a marble palace in the midst of a flower garden, and he lived there happily.

His wife, however, had not given birth to any children, and for the couple this was a great sorrow.

One day, an old woman knocked at the door and begged for something to eat. The sailor's wife was kind to her, but in spite of this, the old woman would not leave.

Then, the sailor's wife said: "Why aren't you leaving? What else do you want from me?"

"Dear lady," the old woman answered, "I know why you are so sad. You do not have any children. But you were good to me, and I want to reward you. Here is an orange. You must eat half of it and your husband must eat the other half. Then, throw the rind under that orange tree that is in the garden."

After saying this, the old woman disappeared.

Nine months later, the sailor's wife gave birth to a beautiful baby. There was great joy in the sailor's mansion, and they celebrated by consuming one thousand wine barrels, three thousand sacks of wheat, three hundred oxen, a large flock of lambs, and I don't even know how many jars of honey.

The baby was named Giuseppe, and when he grew up and became a young man, he had a strong body and a love for weapons. Consequently, his father gave him a sword as a present.

One day, Giuseppe descended into the garden to test his sword. When he struck a fig tree with his new sword, it shattered into one hundred pieces. Giuseppe then bent over the ground and began to gather the pieces. As he reached the orange tree, where his mother had long ago thrown the orange rind, he saw a hilt embedded in the foot of the tree. He grabbed it and began to pull. He pulled and pulled, and finally a shiny blade came out. So, Giuseppe took this sword and struck the fig tree a second time, and this time the sword was severed in two.

Now, the sailor's son was good and handsome, but he always had to be busy and do new things. Finally, he had the idea of traveling the world in search of fortune. His mother and father were unable to change his mind, and so he left. After a long journey, he arrived at a town where he met a man who was walking with an aristocratic demeanor.

The man asked him, "What are you doing?"

"I am traveling the world."

"If you come with me, I'll treat you with great kindness and pay you well. What's more, I'll only order you to do something once a year."

"Yes," Giuseppe agreed, and away they went.

One day, the man said to him, "Prepare the horses. We have something to do."

They went on their way and reached the bottom of a mountain that touched the clouds and shone like an endless treasure.

"Now, get off and kill one of the horses."

So, Giuseppe dismounted and killed one of the horses.

"Take off the horse's skin," the man said.

Giuseppe took off the skin, and then the man said, "Wrap yourself in that skin."

Giuseppe wrapped himself in the skin, and all of a sudden, a flock of birds flew down and grabbed him, lifting him up in the air to the top of a mountain that was made entirely of gold and gemstones.

The man shouted: "Now that you are at the top, roll all those gold stones down to me."

Giuseppe began to roll down the gold stones, and after he had been working for a while, the man shouted: "That's enough! Now try to come down as best you can."

Giuseppe tried to come down, but in vain. There were ravines on one side and cliffs on the other. He didn't even know where to set his foot. Finally, just as night was falling, he found a path lined with rosebushes. At the end of the path, Giuseppe found a fountain, and next to the fountain there was an old man sitting on the ground.

Giuseppe told him, "Please teach me the way to go back down to the plain." Then Giuseppe added, "Around here, there are only cliffs."

"I don't know," the old man answered.

"Then what am I supposed to do?"

"I can tell you that every day, three doves come here. Whoever catches one of those doves can go back down."

It was nighttime, and since Giuseppe was very tired, he fell asleep under the bushes. At dawn he awoke and lay in wait. The doves came down, and he captured one, which immediately turned into a maiden. (The three doves were the daughters of a king, and the one that had turned into a maiden was not even the most beautiful of the three.)

Together with the maiden, Giuseppe started toward the house of the Wizard, who reigned over the mountain. The maiden told him: "We have to find out what we must do to kill the Wizard."

At night, at the Wizard's house, everyone sat down to eat and began to chat cheerfully. Through subtle tricks, the maiden managed to discover what she needed to know. "At the top of another mountain lives a porcupine that eats people with his eyes," she told Giuseppe. "Whoever kills him will find a hare in his belly. Whoever kills the hare will find a dove, and then inside the dove, an egg. If the Wizard is hit on his forehead with that egg, he will die."

As soon as he heard this, Giuseppe left the maiden and told her, "I am going to kill the porcupine."

So, he set off. Along the way, he met a lion, an ant, and a dove: the three animals were fighting over the carcass of an animal.

The ant said: "Let us call this man and let him divvy up the portions."

Giuseppe wisely put the meat for the dove in one place, and in another place the bones for the lion, and in a third spot he placed the head for the ant, who could also find shelter there.

Everyone was satisfied, so they said, "Now we want to reward you."

The dove plucked out one of its feathers, gave it to him, and said: "If you have need for it, you may shout, 'I am a man. Let me become a dove.' And right away you will become a dove. And then, again, if you say, 'I am a dove. Let me become a man,' you will become a man again."

The lion gave him a tuft of his fur to become a lion, and the ant also taught him a way to become an ant.

Giuseppe set off on his journey with these gifts. At sunset, he arrived at a farmhouse and asked for hospitality.

The farmer asked him, "What are you up to?"

"I am traveling the world."

"Do you want to stay with me as a watchman? I will have you guard the sheep."

Giuseppe agreed.

"But be careful not to let them graze beyond that mountain. The porcupine lives up there. He will eat both you and the sheep."

Giuseppe answered, "Very well, master. Leave it to me."

At dawn, he drove the sheep in front of him and slowly approached the mountain, where the pastures were rich and green. The sheep were grazing peacefully, when, all of a sudden, the porcupine showed up and grabbed one of them

Giuseppe took out the tuft of fur and shouted, "I am a man. Let me become a lion!"

And, as a lion, he attacked the porcupine. He fought at length but was unable to kill the monster, who defended himself savagely.

Since he was now exhausted, he took out the feather and shouted, "I am a man. Let me become a dove!"

Then he flew off to rest in the branches of an oak tree. A little later, before the monster regained his strength, he became a lion again and won the fight. Once more, Giuseppe regained his true form, cut open the porcupine's belly, found the hare, and killed it. All at once, a dove emerged from the dead hare. He grabbed the dove, choked it, opened it, and found the egg. He put the egg in his pocket and left for the farmhouse with the sheep.

Once he arrived there, he told the farmer: "Now you may send your sheep to graze on the mountain without fear. I killed the porcupine and lost only one sheep."

The farmer could not believe that Giuseppe had killed such a terrifying beast. But as soon as he made certain that was indeed the case, he begged the young man: "Stay with me until death. I will give you whatever you want."

Giuseppe answered: "I have business to take care of. So, I must leave."

And he left.

Soon he arrived at the Wizard's house. The large house looked like a monastery: all the windows and all the doors were shut. A deep silence filled the air. As soon as the porcupine had been killed, the Wizard had begun to feel sick. His strength had abated, his shoulders slumped, and his beard had grown white. "My days are over!" he moaned.

Afterward, he lay down on the bed. Then, he ordered the house to be shut, so he could defend himself from death.

When Giuseppe saw the house closed and impenetrable, he shouted, "I am a man. Let me become an ant."

He entered the room where the Wizard was suffering. And all of a sudden, after he became a man again, he threw the egg at the Wizard's forehead, causing him to fall down dead. At that point, the walls of the house disappeared, as if by magic. Out of the foundations grew trees, trees, and more trees, and they spread all around and covered many square miles of land.

The new forest was quite treacherous, and not many humans could get through it. However, Giuseppe was able to cross it—by turns becoming an ant, or a lion, or a dove. He moved toward the fountain, and there he found the three doves that had turned into maidens. He joined them, and together they all traveled toward his father's kingdom.

The king wanted to give Giuseppe the most beautiful of the girls as a wife, but Giuseppe married the one who had been grabbed at the edge of the fountain. She was not that beautiful, but she was very loving.

The Song of the Bloodied Ricotta
(Land of Abruzzi—Aquila)

There once was a queen whose only son did not want to take a wife because in his entire kingdom, he could not find a woman as beautiful as he desired. The queen was afflicted by this, and so she summoned to the palace all the young women she could find. They came from many cities and from every social rank, but none of them enticed the prince. Still, the queen wanted her son to marry at all costs.

One day, at the dinner table, the queen was about to slice a fragrant fresh ricotta, but as soon as she started to slice it, she cut her finger, and the ricotta reddened with blood.

"Dear mother," said the prince, "you want me to take a wife, right? Well, if I find a woman as white and red as that ricotta, I will marry her."

"My dear son, take a horse and a bag full of gold, and set off for foreign lands. That is how you will perhaps find her."

The prince took the horse and the bag full of gold and left on his journey. After he had gone a long way, he began to get frustrated because he could not find the beautiful woman he had been dreaming of. Eventually, at the border with the kingdom of Naples, he met an elderly beggar, who stopped him and asked, "O handsome youth, where are you going?"

"Well, kind woman, I am going about my business."

"If you tell me what you are looking for, I may be able to help you."

"Kind woman, I am looking for a bride who is as white and red as this ricotta."

And he showed her the ricotta that his mother had entrusted to him before his departure.

"I have wandered far and searched very hard, but I have not yet found her. Kind woman, I have lost hope, and so I am going back home."

"Is this what is troubling you? I will help you, then. Here are three walnuts. When you come across a fountain, you will break one walnut, and a beautiful maiden will come to life, white and red like that ricotta. But she will be naked. You must be quick to cover her with a cloak, otherwise she will vanish. If she vanishes the first time, then when you come across a second fountain, you will break another walnut, and another maiden, equally beautiful, will appear before you. If this one should also vanish because you are too slow to cover her with a cloak, then, as soon as you come across a third fountain, you will open the third walnut, and a maiden as beautiful as her companions will appear before you. But watch out! This time, throw a cloak upon her quick as a flash because, if you let this one also disappear, I will no longer be able to help you."

"Thank you, kind woman."

The prince took the three walnuts from the beggar, and rewarded her with a handful of gold coins.

As soon as he arrived at the first fountain, he broke a walnut, following the instructions he was given, and immediately a beautiful maiden appeared: she was stark naked, and white and red like the ricotta. But the prince was not quick enough to throw a cloak upon her, and to his great sorrow, she disappeared.

After another journey, the prince came across a second fountain. He broke the other walnut, and another maiden came out, more beautiful than the first. But he was not quick enough in throwing a cloak upon her this time either, and thus he was left empty-handed.

He started back on his path, thinking that now he only had one walnut left, and that if this last time he was not careful, he would lose his good fortune forever.

He came across the third fountain, and there he broke the third walnut, and this time he managed to throw a cloak upon the naked maiden just in time, and she did not disappear.

She was more beautiful than the other two and the prince could not get enough of looking at her. However, now he had to run and fetch some clothes to get her dressed.

"O beauty," he said, "climb atop that tree, and I will go fetch your clothes and return to you within three days. Be careful! Don't listen to anyone."

Now, let's leave the prince, who went to buy gifts for his bride and prepare the celebrations for their wedding. The next morning, one of the queen's servants came to draw water from the fountain, located just under the tree where the maiden had climbed. Reflected in the water, the servant saw the image of the beautiful woman hidden among the branches. Believing that to be her own reflection, the servant started saying: "I am so very beautiful! Why should I have to go and draw water with a pitcher?" So, she tossed the pitcher to the ground and left.

The next morning, the same thing happened.

The third morning, the servant looked up into the tree and realized that the reflection in the water belonged to the mysterious maiden.

"Goodness, what a beautiful lady! What are you doing up there? Come down, I want to comb your hair. Look at how disheveled you are!"

The beautiful maiden did not want to come down, but the servant managed to convince her. While combing her hair, the servant stuck a pin in her head, and the beautiful maiden suddenly turned into a dove and flew away.

That evil servant, knowing that the maiden in the branches was actually waiting for the prince, got undressed, wrapped herself in the maiden's cloak, and climbed atop the tree.

The prince returned, and as soon as he saw the ugly servant, he was befuddled and did not know what to say. He eventually regained his composure and asked: "How did you become so ugly when you used to be more beautiful than the sun?"

"Ah, my lord, the air and the light offend me. Let me rest for eight days in a dark room, and then you shall see how I will regain all my beauty."

"Let's hope so," answered the prince, and he led her to the palace.

Once there, he immediately shut her in a dark room, and told the queen the news.

"Mother, let eight days go by, and then you shall see."

Eight days went by, but the bride was still ugly.

"Sire, marry me now, because with time I will become beautiful again. Have no fear."

And the entire kingdom celebrated their wedding with much joy. Cooks of great repute came from all over the world to prepare the marriage banquet and worked under the orders of a master chef. While the cooks were getting the food ready, a beautiful dove landed on a windowsill and started singing.

> O cook, cook of the great kitchen,
> What is the king doing with that ugly Saracen?
> May sleep overtake you at the stove
> And may all the food burn!

The chef fell asleep and the food burned. When he awoke and saw what happened, the poor chef was overtaken with despair. Nevertheless, he fixed the dishes as best he could and had them brought to the dinner table.

The king was furious and began to shout, "Why is all the food burnt? Why?"

"Your Majesty, forgive me this time! Sleep overtook me."

But the next day, the dove returned.

O cook, cook of the great kitchen,
What is the king doing with that ugly Saracen?
May sleep overtake you at the stove
And may all the food burn!

And so it was. That morning, the king did not want to hear any excuses, so the poor chef decided he would tell him the truth. Thus, taking the king aside, he told him: "Your Majesty, every morning, while I am cooking, a dove comes to the kitchen and tells me this:

O cook, cook of the great kitchen,
What is the king doing with that ugly Saracen?
May sleep overtake you at the stove
And may all the food burn!

Then the dove flies away, and I fall asleep."

The king said: "Tomorrow come and get me, and together we will try to catch that dove."

The following morning, as the hour of the dove's appearance drew near, the chef had the king called over. The dove flew down.

O cook, cook of the great kitchen . . .

The king approached the dove very carefully and managed to take her prisoner. Then, after petting her a while, he shut her inside a golden cage.

The next day, while the chef was admiring the dove, he noticed that she had a pin stuck in her head. He delicately pulled out the pin, and all of a sudden, the dove turned back into a beautiful woman, as if by magic.

The chef ran to tell the king, and the king immediately recognized the woman he loved.

"Dear bride! You are my bride! Tell me what happened! Please tell me what happened!"

"Right now, I cannot tell you anything. But bring me with you to the dinner table and announce that I am a foreigner. Then, toward the end of the meal, make sure that everyone is asked to tell a fairy tale."

"All right," answered the king.

As soon as she saw that beautiful lady at the dinner table, the ugly woman felt her veins freeze, and was no longer able to utter a single word. Nevertheless, she kept quiet.

Toward the end of the meal, the king said: "Now everyone must tell a fairy tale, and the foreign lady shall go first."

Everyone agreed: "Yes, yes: the foreign lady shall go first."

Only the ugly woman was quiet.

So, the foreign lady began: "Once upon a time, there was a maiden on top of a tree, waiting for the prince her bridegroom. An ugly servant came to draw water at the fountain, under that very tree, and . . ." and she proceeded to tell the entire story of her encounter with the Saracen woman.

When she was done with her story, everyone asked at the same time "What punishment would Your Ladyship give that evil impostor?"

"I would make her wear a shirt soaked in pitch and have her burned in the middle of the square."

The king stood up and began shouting: "The shirt soaked in pitch is ready, and so is the impostor."

He called the guards, ordered them to tie up the ugly Saracen, put the shirt on her, and set it alight. And the king and his bride, along with the courtiers, stood at their balconies enjoying the spectacle. He then announced the wedding throughout his provinces, and the celebrations were marvelous and lasted many days and many nights without a break.

The Borea's Daughter

I.

King Caldore and Queen Olina were well into their old age. Their court was made up of wise knights, monks, astrologers, and alchemists, with whom the royals enjoyed conversing about philosophical matters, learning the doctrine of the stars, interpreting the Sacred Scriptures, and studying the virtues of metals and stones according to the Lapidary of Bishop Marbod. Their faces were grave and majestic, their white hair was most pure, their voices were sweet. Although their movements were slow, they carried themselves with much grace. Whenever they rode over the gentle hills of their kingdom, men humbly hastened to pay them homage and women scattered an abundance of flowers on their path.

Their son was a handsome and well-built prince, and the queen used to often tell him: "My son, we are old now. Why don't you choose a bride for yourself?" At her words, the prince became thoughtful, and sometimes sighed from the bottom of his heart.

One day, because it was the Christian Feast of the Ascension, the valets brought a fresh white *giuncata* cheese to the rose-strewn tables. While the prince was cutting it with a golden knife, he wounded his hand, and a drop of blood stained the milky whiteness of the cheese.

"Dear mother," the prince said, smiling, "I will gladly choose a bride, but I would like her to look like this: blood and milk."

A light murmuring spread across the tables, like a wind among the branches, and the maidens blushed.

The prince added, "I shall find her."

The next day, he went to his father and mother, and said, "Give me your holy blessing." After he received their blessing, he set out on his path.

He traveled all day, going through woods and rivers without ever stopping. Night overtook him in the middle of an endless plain. It was a moonless night, and when the prince glimpsed in the wilderness a spot shining like a star, his heart started beating faster: the more he advanced, the brighter that spot became. Finally, the prince arrived in the vicinity of a grand palace and set his foot within a circle of light.

The splendor of the palace could be seen within a seven-mile radius: it was bathed in daylight, while the surrounding lands lay in darkness. The palace rose on a riverbank, near lush mazes filled with deer and peacocks. Its white marble architecture rose up toward the sky and four stairways, flanked by banisters, descended into the river. In the sparkling clear waters, one could see the steps reach the bottom of a riverbed made of golden sand.

On the other shore, there was a great forest thick with foliage. From the trees next to the riverbank dripped an abundance of liquid sap, which flowed from the trunks into the water and formed golden clumps of amber carried away by the current. The reflections of the palace and the trees seemed to embrace one another on the gently rippling water. Everything was serene.

The prince paused, overtaken by wonder. Then he took courage and cried out from the bottom of the palace.

"Who is calling?" asked the beautiful Vienda, looking out from the balcony of a tall and secluded tower.

"For the love of Our Lord Jesus Christ, give me shelter, beautiful maiden. I am a poor traveler," pleaded the prince.

"Go away! Go away! My mother is not with me."

"Have pity, beautiful maiden. I am dying of fatigue and hunger."

"Go away! Go away! My mother is not with me."

"Be merciful, for the love of the Mother of God, beautiful maiden. My knees are giving out, my feet are bleeding."

"Go away, go away!"

"O beautiful maiden, who gave you such a hard heart? Look at me from your balcony and watch me die."

"God! God!"

Trembling, Vienda came down the tower and opened the door.

The prince cried out in the presence of her great beauty.

"Mother of God, dear Mother of God, let us thank the Lord Our God, because I have found my bride."

"Who are you?" asked Vienda, as soon as she saw the young stranger. "Come in and hide. If my mother returns, she will devour you."

"I am the son of a king, and I was searching for you. For pity's sake, do not send me away!"

Vienda closed the door, which at the touch of her hand sparkled like a diamond in a ray of sunshine. Then she led the prince up the stairway inside.

II.

The stairs wound in long spires around a tall column, like snakes twisted around a rod. The column was made of a magical stone and held up the whole building. It produced a wondrous light that could go through any matter, creating a circle of brightness around itself for exactly seven miles. Like the flame in a crystal lamp, so was the column in the turreted castle.

Once she reached her tower, Vienda told the prince, "Come in, my lord."

This is where the beautiful woman lived, and where she enjoyed quilting vestments and stoles, sitting on silver brocade cushions like the women of the Orient, and resting from her gentle labor by praying to God. The gemstones on the walls lit up the room. Aloe burned in a vase and gave out its scent. Dressed in Catura silk, Vienda quilted and sang. Her movements were harmonious as music, and her entire body radiated light and youth, like the body of a goddess. She quilted as she sang, and the combination of light, scents, movements, and voice formed a sort of spell around her.

"Come in, my lord."

The prince went in.

"Sit down, my lord."

The prince sat down.

Vienda moved to the balcony and paused for a moment, listening. The silence was deep, on that magical day.

"O beautiful maiden," asked the prince, "would you like me to be your bridegroom?"

"I would like that very much, my lord. But you must know that my mother is the Borea, and if she returns, she will surely devour you."

"You will save me, beautiful maiden, because you are my bride."

Anxiety appeared in Vienda's eyes just as they heard a distant noise coming from the forest on the other side of the shore. The noise rapidly grew louder: it was like the bellowing of a great wind.

"Here comes my mother!" the beautiful maiden exclaimed.

The entire forest roared, along with the river.

"Here comes my mother!"

The entire forest roared, and the palace trembled from its very foundations.

"Here comes my mother! Hide inside that gold coffer."

The prince hid inside the gold coffer.

The wind beat the walls hard, beating and beating so as to assume once again a human shape. Finally, after the transformation was completed, the Borea called from below the tower:

> *Vienda, my daughter, O flower of beauty,*
> *come to the balcony, spread out your braids!*
> *Spread out your beautiful braids, eye of the sun,*
> *because your mother wants to come up.*
> *She wants to come up on the sweet ladder:*
> *come to the balcony, let down your beautiful braids!*
> *She wants to come up on that ladder of gold:*
> *Vienda, my daughter, let down your treasure!*

From the top of the tower, Vienda let down her long hair, and the Borea climbed up. As soon as she was inside, the Borea sniffed at the air. Vienda threw a handful of pure aloe into the burning brazier, but in vain. The Borea said, "There is a human being in here."

"Dear mother, how could a human possibly come up here? Maybe you still have their scent in your nostrils because you have traveled all over the world."

The Borea did not desist and searched throughout the tower, until she finally found the king's son, hidden inside the precious coffer.

"Ah, it is you here? Get ready to die," she said, as her teeth made a terrible screeching sound.

"Forgive him, mother," Vienda begged, kneeling. "He is a traveler who has lost his way and is asking for shelter for this night only."

The Borea forgave him, for that night only.

III.

The next morning, before leaving, the Borea called the king's son, who was still asleep.

"Get up and follow me," she said.

The prince got up and followed her into a large room made entirely of crystal, where an enormous pile of gems blazed like fire. There were over a hundred sacks of emeralds, sapphires, garnets, chrysocollas, almandines, hyacinths, and turquoises, and they shone so brightly that the prince was overwhelmed by their radiance and almost lost his mind.

"I am shutting you up in this room," the Borea said. "By tonight, upon my return, all the stones must be separated into seven piles according to their kind. If not, prepare to die."

She locked the door and left for her mysterious travels across land and sea.

When the king's son heard the forest roar like the previous night, he imagined he would receive a terrible punishment. The pile of gems in the middle of the sparkling floor flashed like flames, waiting for him to get to work. A deep silence filled the house.

"Jesus Christ, help me!" prayed the wretched prince. And as he looked at the pile, which would require at least one month to be counted by a single man, he broke down crying.

"Dear Vienda! Dear Vienda, my bride!"

The maiden appeared on the other side of the translucent and echoing wall. She was smiling, and her smile multiplied on the gems like a glittering wave on a calm lake.

Three times she circled silently around the prince's prison, and then she spoke.

"Do not cry, bridegroom of mine. The gems will obey me: I know them well."

Now the stones started to shine more brightly and to come alive, just like eyes that were seeing for the first time.

Vienda called the garnets: "Dear garnets, you who have the power to comfort men's bodies and souls, to chase away sadness and vain dreams forever. . . . I order you to separate from the others."

At those words, the garnets rushed out of the pile, like the sparks of a fire in a sudden wind.

She called the sapphires: "Dear sapphires, gems fit for the fingers of kings, with the power to quench human thirst, relieve inner fevers, heal wounds when infused in milk, and protect chaste men against fear, against betrayal, and against poison. . . . I order you to separate from the others."

The sapphires came out of the pile and, no longer disturbed by the other flames, shone placidly, all together on the same side, like fragments of a clear sky.

She called the emeralds: "Dear emeralds, custodians of chastity, healers of leprosy, you discover lies, increase wealth, calm every storm. . . . I order you to separate from the others."

The emeralds came out of the pile, like tiny leaves on a trunk soaked through at springtime.

She then called the chrysocollas, the almandines, the hyacinths, the turquoises. At her words, all the different types of gems separated before the astonished prince.

IV.

That night, when the Borea came home and saw that the stones had been successfully separated into piles, she said: "This is not your work, but my daughter Vienda's."

And the next day, before leaving the house, she led the prince to another large room, where a pile of feathers lay on the floor, cheery and soft like a harvest of flowers.

"One hundred kinds of birds have provided these feathers," said the Borea. "You must now separate the one hundred types into one hundred different piles. If not, prepare to die."

And she left the house, growling.

At that point, Vienda opened the door to the prison with a magic trick and presented herself before the king's son, who was weeping.

"I do not weep for fear of death, but because you will no longer be my bride!"

"I will be your bride because I love you. Do you want to run away with me, my lord?"

"I do."

"Well, then, just wait."

Before running away, Vienda prepared a potion and gave it to all the objects in the house, since they were enchanted. But she forgot to give some to a golden trivet sitting amid the ashes.

"Are you ready?" the impatient prince asked.

"Here I am. Wait a minute."

She took a comb, a shuttle, and a relic of the Cross of Our Lord Jesus Christ, and then cried, "Let's go!"

She led her lover through a maze of stairways and to a sturdy cedarwood door. Immediately, the door obeyed Vienda's whispered command and opened onto an enclosed yard. Flowering rosebushes grew all around, forming an impenetrable barrier. The ground was covered with soft grass, gleaming with dew, and streams of water irrigated the greenery while making a soft music. It is here that the Borea's horses were grazing.

They were white as swans, lean as unicorns, fierce as sphynxes, and fiery as chimeras. Their eyes shone black and wet among their manes, which were so long that their galloping legs got tangled in them, and their legs ended in hooves as polished as jasper, producing sparks and thunder as they went. When the horses heard the beautiful maiden cry for them softly, they ran over to her neighing and quivering, asking to run, placing the breath of their nostrils on her hands, begging with their eyes for endless open spaces. Vienda chose the two fastest runners from among the herd and leaped onto one as the prince leaped on the other. As soon as they felt the riders' weight on them, the horses took off like arrows from a bow.

V.

That evening, the Borea came home and called out:

> *Vienda, my daughter, o flower of beauty,*
> *come to the balcony, spread out your braids!*
> *Spread out your beautiful braids, eye of the sun,*
> *because your mother wants to come up.*
> *She wants to come up on the sweet ladder:*
> *come to the balcony, let down your beautiful braids!*
> *She wants to come up on that ladder of gold:*
> *Vienda, my daughter, let down your treasure!*

She called at length and in vain: no one appeared on the balcony of the tower. But the golden trivet, which had not been given potion to drink, slowly approached a window and said, "Don't bother calling, because your Vienda has run off with the king's son."

The Borea let out a scream, and without delay set off to follow the fugitives. She ran, and ran, and ran, and Vienda heard her from afar.

"Here comes my mother! Here comes my mother!" said Vienda, and she tossed the shuttle.

"I wish for this shuttle to become a mountain as tall as the clouds, so that not even the wind can get across it."

The shuttle became a mountain, but the Borea, after much effort, managed to cross it.

"Here comes my mother! Here comes my mother!"

Vienda tossed the comb.

"I wish for this comb to become a thorn bush so thick that not even the wind can penetrate it."

The comb became a thorn bush. The Borea got all bloodied, but went through it.

"Here comes my mother! Here comes my mother!" said Vienda, and she tossed the relic. The relic became a church, Vienda became a holy water font, the king's son became a crucifix, and the horses disappeared.

The mother arrived at the church and entered it. A solemn silence reigned inside, and within the chapels there were fragrant lamps burning to light the holy images on the walls. The entire nave of the church was reflected in the deep baptismal font. The Borea stopped and listened, but she could hear only her own wheezing. She then kneeled in the middle of the church, took out her breasts, let down her hair, and swore: "Dear daughter, I do not curse you. But may your bridegroom, as soon as he receives his mother's first kiss, forget all about you for seven years."

The Borea kissed the floor and left, so Vienda and her bridegroom returned to their human form and went back on their way. After many miles, they arrived at a place not far from the city, with a spring of pure water in the shade of a tall willow tree.

The prince said, "I do not want you to enter the city without celebration. Let me go ahead and arrange the ceremonies, while you wait for me here. Actually, so that no one may see you, go ahead and hide in this willow tree, among the weeping branches reflected in the fountain."

"Are you abandoning me?" said Vienda. "You must remember the curse: if your mother kisses you, I will remain here for seven years, forgotten."

"Do not fear, my beautiful maiden. I will not let myself be kissed."

"You must remember!"

"I will not let myself be kissed."

The prince went back to his father's royal palace, while the beautiful Vienda remained on the willow tree.

As soon as the prince set foot on the threshold of the royal palace, a loud clamor of joy suddenly spread throughout the hallways, rooms, and gardens. The queen mother ran toward her beloved son, and before he was able to defend himself from her ardor, she threw her arms around him and covered his face with kisses.

The king's son forgot all about Vienda.

At length, Vienda waited, within the willow tree, and when she saw that her bridegroom was not coming back, she told herself, weeping, "His mother kissed him!"

So, she stayed for seven years in the willow tree, weeping.

VI.

At the end of seven years, a little woman came with a clay pitcher to draw water from the fountain. It was a springtime day, and the green fronds of the willow tree hung freely to the ground, mixed with the hair of the abandoned Vienda.

The little woman saw Vienda's beautiful face reflected in the water, and believing that to be her own reflection, she exclaimed, "Look at how beautiful I am!" And she stared and marveled for a while, astonished.

"How is it possible that I am so beautiful and still must draw water? Cursed be the mistress who sent me!"

And she tossed the clay pitcher, which broke into a thousand pieces. At that, Vienda laughed out loud from the top of the tree. The little woman heard the laughter, raised her eyes, and exclaimed, "Ah, it is you, beautiful lady!"

The lady was laughing at the top of the willow tree, like the sun at the top of a hill, and amid the weeping branches her hair, turned wild, looked like golden rays.

"Good maiden," the wind's daughter said, "do me a service. Go to the king's son and tell him that for seven years already I have been forgotten in this willow tree."

"O beautiful lady, why don't you come down? You are as beautiful as the sun, but your hair is so unkempt. I want to comb it. Come down!"

"I cannot come down, good maiden, because my hair is braided together with the branches of the willow tree, like golden thread in silken ropes."

"O beautiful lady, I want to comb your hair: shame on you for being so unkempt. Come down!"

"I cannot come down, good maiden. The branches tie my wrists and ankles."

"Come down!"

Vienda, who liked the idea of being freed from the tree's tangles, leapt to the ground, breaking every tie. Her hair, strewn with green leaves, covered her completely, like a cloth stitched with fine gemstones.

"Sit on that rock, beautiful lady," the little woman told her.

Vienda sat on the rock, and the other woman, who was sitting at the edge of the fountain, said, "Rest your head on my knees."

Vienda rested her beautiful head on the knees of the woman, who began to comb her hair. Under the bite of the comb, the leaves fell off Vienda's hair one by one.

"Why don't you tell me your story, my lady, while I comb your hair?"

Vienda began to tell her story, and although one could not see her face, hidden as it was by her hair, nor her speaking mouth, still her sweet speech seemed to gently flow from all that blondness, much like a vein of water springs shyly yet brightly from among the soft green grass around it.

As soon as Vienda finished the story, she was about to raise her head, but the evil woman took the golden hairpin that Vienda was wearing and pierced her delicate temple with it. Vienda died, without a sigh. One single drop of blood flowed out of her wound and fell on a flower: the flower turned into a dove, and the dove right away took flight.

The evil woman took the corpse's clothes, wore them, and threw the body into the nearby fishpond. Then, she climbed up the willow tree. To the women who came to draw water, she said: "Go to the king's son and tell him that I have been here in this willow tree for seven years already, forgotten."

VII.

The women went to call the king's son.

"Ah, what a scoundrel I have been!" cried the prince, beating his forehead. "My poor bride!"

He gathered the entire court, as well as the army—both infantry and knights—and ordered a celebration of unprecedented magnificence.

The royal parade passed under flower garlands and over flower carpets. The horses had bridles embroidered with pearls and wore shimmery caparisons, the edges of which were held up by green-clad dwarves who carried ivory trumpets on their backs. One hundred damsels and one hundred pageboys sang beautiful melodies. Forty white hackneys were loaded with great treasures destined to adorn the princess Blood-and-Milk. The entire population followed, shouting with joy.

When the parade arrived at the willow over the fountain, the king's son ran ahead. But when he saw the little woman dressed in Vienda's clothes, he exclaimed, stunned, "God! How different you are!" And he was befuddled.

"Ah, I am different, am I?" she answered, in a harsh voice. "The sun burned me, the rain drenched me to the bones, the ice has frozen me, for seven years!"

The prince felt his heart tighten with remorse.

"For seven years! The sun has blackened me, the rain has shrunken me, the ice has made me ill, for seven years!"

The prince stretched his arms out to her. "My poor bride!"

VIII.

Their return was triumphant, celebrated with an abundance of roses and musical instruments playing sublime songs. But the people said, looking at the new princess: "This, then, is the famous Blood-and-Milk? This, then, is the beauty of beauties? This is the fiancée who comes from afar?"

The court poets worked hard to find rhymes of praise, but their words showed very little passion, and the aristocratic ladies laughed cruelly, looking at the rough and ugly face of the false Vienda.

The wedding feast was ready, and the princes, dukes, counts, barons—in short, all the gravest lords of the realm—were sitting at the dinner table. The servants brought steaming peacocks on silver bowls, with their feathers still in place, and the cup bearers poured rivulets of wine from alabaster urns into agate goblets. Musicians played and dancers danced to cheer up everyone's heart.

The mother queen gently leaned toward her son and asked him: "Remember, dear son, that drop of blood that fell on the cheese and gave you the desire for a bride who was Blood-and-Milk?"

As soon as the drop of blood was mentioned, a snow-white dove came in through a balcony, descended on the table, and started moaning sweetly.

"Kill that dove!" cried the false princess as she got up suddenly, pale and dismayed.

The king's son took out his sword and killed the dove in flight, but from the dove's death a human life appeared: it was Vienda's shape, the beautiful Blood-and-Milk, and she lit up the entire party, like a sunrise.

Overtaken by marvel, all present were silent.

"Here is your bride!" sang the Borea's daughter, stretching her arms out to the prince. "Here is the bride who died for you and for you is alive again."

The prince ran into her arms and said, "Here is your bridegroom, my queen!"

Then the Borea's daughter kissed the mouth of the king's son, so that she was forever his.

All around, the cries and greetings multiplied, as flower petals rained down on everyone and rivers of wine flowed freely. The evil woman was burned alive, in front of the balconies of the royal palace, and the flames made the crockery and cups of the party sparkle once again.

Our Lady of Good Counsel

Today, my young friends, I want to tell you a story that will move you deeply, and if it does not move you, it will certainly not be because of me, nor because of the things I tell you, but because you have a heart of stone.

Once upon a time, in a village of Sardinia through which you have never traveled and likely never will, there lived a very evil man, who did not believe in God, and who never gave alms to the poor. This man's name was Don Juanne Perez. He was of Spanish origin and was as ugly as the devil. He lived in a huge house, dark and mysterious, made up of one hundred and one rooms, and kept with him a fifteen-year-old niece named Mariedda as a servant.

Mariedda was as good, beautiful, and devout as her uncle was evil, ugly, and godless. Mariedda had the prettiest black hair in all of Sardinia, and one of her eyes looked like the morning star and the other like the evening star. Don Juanne hated Mariedda, just like he hated every human being on this earth, and, if he could, he would have plucked out her big, beautiful eyes, but as a last matter of conscience, he did not want to hurt her. Still, when she turned fifteen, he thought he would get rid of her by marrying her off to an ugly man in the village. Mariedda, however, did not consent to this unhappy marriage. One night, the ugly villager, to take revenge on her humiliating rejection, uprooted all the plants in Don Juanne's garden and placed a pair of horns and two enormous pumpkins on the threshold of the house where Mariedda lived with her uncle. And every night, he walked under the windows singing evil songs.

It's impossible to describe just how angry Don Juanne became, or the aversion he began to feel against poor Mariedda from that moment on. Suffice it to say that one day he took her with him to the most remote room in the house and told her: "You did not want Predu Concaepreda [Peter Head of Stone] as a husband. Well, then, since you absolutely must marry, get ready to marry me instead."

The poor girl was petrified, and exclaimed: "But how is that even possible? Aren't you my uncle? And since when can uncles marry their own nieces?"

"You be quiet, you little flirt! I have permission from the pope to marry whomever I want, and to get married even without a priest. And I have decided to take whomever I please as a wife. Mind your own business, then. It's either that man from the village or me. I'll give you one night to decide."

And he left her locked in her room. As soon as she was alone, Mariedda started crying and praying fervently to Our Lady of Good Counsel to help and inspire her. And just look! As soon as night fell, a beautiful lady appeared to her, enveloped in light, dressed in satin and a white veil, with a blue mantle and a golden tiara like the one worn by the Queen of Spain. How did she get in? Mariedda could not explain it, and as she stared open-mouthed at the beautiful Lady, who told her with a voice that sounded like violin music: "I am Our Lady of Good Counsel, and I heard your prayer. Listen, Mariedda: Ask your uncle for an eight-day reprieve, and if at the end of those eight days he has not given up his evil plan, call me again. Keep yourself good, always, and you will always have my help and my counsel."

After she said this, she disappeared, leaving a light like the moon's and a scent of jasmine behind her.

Feeling a great joy, Mariedda prayed all night, and the next day she asked her uncle for an eight-day reprieve. Half-heartedly, Don Juanne agreed. Meanwhile, to make sure that she did not escape, he kept her locked up in that remote room, where the moonlight and jasmine scent still lingered. Once the eight days were over, however, he asked her if she had made up her mind, because he absolutely wanted to marry her the next day.

Once alone, Mariedda started crying and praying again, and soon that Celestial Lady reappeared. She was now wearing a gold brocade dress and a pearl tiara like the one worn by the Queen of France.

"Sleep, Mariedda, and don't be afraid," she said, with a voice that sounded like a nightingale's song. "Take this rosary, which has the virtue of healing the sick, and in your fortune do not forget me, if you don't want misfortune to befall you." Then, she disappeared, leaving in the room the light of a springtime dawn and the fragrance of carnations. Mariedda was unable to say a single word. Hopeful and ecstatic, she kissed the mother-of-pearl rosary left behind by the divine Lady, placed it around her neck, and fell asleep calmly without wondering what might happen the next day.

The following morning, she woke up under a thorn bush, near a swamp, and she immediately thought that her Holy Protectress must have transported her there while she slept. She got up, recited her usual prayers, and then set out toward a city she could see in the distance, amid the rosy mist of the beautiful morning. She walked and walked and saw a young fisherman, who was going to fish in some small blue ponds nearby, barefoot and with his fishing rod on his shoulder.

"Good fisherman," she asked, "please, what is the name of that city?" The fisherman did not answer, and instead started singing:

I fish for eel and hunt geese.
That yonder city is named Othoca.

"Well," Mariedda thought, "we are in Oristano"—for Othoca was Oristano's ancient name. She walked and walked and entered the city, and, immediately, she started looking for a home where she could work as a servant, but in vain. After three days and three nights of going in one door and out another, starving and exhausted, Mariedda had not yet found work. But she did not despair, and she prayed and prayed always to the beautiful Lady of Good Counsel, asking for her help.

Now, on the fourth day, as she was walking in front of the royal palace, Mariedda saw many people speaking softly, their faces pale and full of sorrow.

"Good soldier," she asked a young man-at-arms who was as sad as the rest of the crowd, "what is happening?"

"The son of Arboréa's Judge is about to die, and no physician can save him anymore."

The Judge was the king of Arboréa, and his son was the best knight in all of Sardinia. Mariedda was shaken by the painful news and was about to say a Hail Mary for the dying prince, when, touching the beads of her rosary, she remembered with joy that her rosary had the virtue of healing the sick. Without saying anything, then, she crossed the crowd and managed to penetrate inside the royal palace. However, a captain of the guards stopped her, arrogantly asking her what she wanted.

"I have come to heal Don Mariano, the sick prince," she humbly replied. "I have a marvelous medicine that heals even the dying."

At those words, the arrogant captain led her to the Judge, an old king whose beard reached his knees. Mariedda had to repeat her words to him. The Judge was moved by the beauty of this unknown young woman more so than by her promise, but he said to her: "Take care, maiden with eyes like stars, for if you are deceiving us, we will chop off your head."

"And if I save the prince?"

"We will give you whatever you want."

After saying this, he himself led Mariedda to the dying prince. His time had come: a few more seconds and all would have been lost. But Don Juanne Perrez's niece placed the rosary around the prince's neck and started to pray fervently, kneeling on the deerskin lying in front of the bed. Then, all those present witnessed an extraordinary miracle, with faces pale and amazed. Don Mariano opened his eyes, his beautiful chestnut eyes with their long lashes. Little by little, his cheeks became rosy like the oleander flowers blooming in the royal gardens, and his forehead began to shine with life. Then he smiled and got up, saying, "Father, I am reborn. Who has saved me?"

The Judge cried with joy, and he cried so much that his beard began dripping tears like a tree soaked through by the rain.

"Here!" he answered, lifting up Mariedda.

"You must be a fairy," said the prince, embracing her. "Your eyes shine like the moon. You will be my bride."

And indeed, she became the Judgess of Arboréa shortly after, just as the new brocade dresses for her arrived from France and Flanders, woven with gold and silver, along with matching veils and mantles. Mariedda was so happy that she began to forget the recommendation of Our Lady of Good Counsel—namely, to pray to her and remember her also in her good fortune. After one year had passed, Mariedda had entirely forgotten her Celestial Protectress. The miraculous rosary hung in the royal chapel, among the other relics, and the Judgess rarely descended to the chapel, spending her time, instead, among parties and hunts, among songs, lutes, and the troubadours' mandolins—none of which was in short supply at the court of the Arboréa.

Now it happened that the Spaniards invaded the kingdom of Arboréa, and Don Mariano, Mariedda's husband, had to leave with his army to defend his land and resist the invaders. He set out and left behind Mariedda, who was about to become the mother of a little prince.

"Farewell, good friend," he said, kissing her forehead, before climbing on his great white horse with its red caparison. "Stay in good spirits, and make sure that upon my return I find a little prince as beautiful and strong as . . ."

". . . as you are, good friend," Lady Mariedda replied, with pride.

During the war, Don Mariano was away for a long time from his capital city, from his elderly father, and from his wife. And Mariedda, a few months after his departure, became the mother of a beautiful little boy. This little boy was all rosy, and his little feet and hands looked like flowers. You must know, however, that there was one who anxiously awaited the day of the beautiful little boy's birth, so as to destroy all the happiness of the Judgess, Lady Mariedda.

It was Don Juanne Perrez.

After the separation from his niece, he had started to hate her fiercely, swearing to take his revenge on her. But no matter how much he searched through the Logudoro and the neighboring lands, no one had ever seen or heard of the starry-eyed girl. As a result of this, Don Juanne was beginning to think, with evil joy, that the devil had taken her away. When he went to Oristano for the celebrations in honor of the prince's wedding, however, he was astonished to see that the bride was Mariedda herself, and he became furious. So, what did he do? He returned to his village, sold all that he owned, and even sold his soul to the devil so that he might get help in his vengeance. He then dressed as a beggar with a long white beard and a long black coat. He dressed this way because he had read in an old book that the ancient physician Claudius Galenus dressed like this. Thus disguised, Don Juanne Perrez set off again for Oristano, pretending to be a physician newly arrived from Germany, and who had studied in Regensburg.

He was so clever with words and deeds that he was accepted as a court physician. Mariedda did not recognize him at all. And when her beautiful little boy was born, the false physician was called. He had been awaiting this opportunity to exact his revenge. After hiding the beautiful little boy, he replaced him cleverly with an ugly and mangy black puppy that he had kept ready for this purpose. He performed this cowardly feat with such skill that not even Mariedda took notice of it. Don Juanne did not kill the beautiful little boy, but let him starve to death. This is why still today in many parts of Sardinia, hunger is called Master Juanne, in remembrance of this fact.

Meanwhile, the Royal Court was steeped in utter grief and fear, because no one had ever seen such a thing. Mariedda herself was feverish with pain and humiliation. It would have been more acceptable had she been an ordinary woman and given birth to a mangy black dog. Good heavens! That would have been acceptable because in those days there were witches who married the devil, and even little dogs and scorpions could be born of these horrific unions. But not of a little Judgess, who wore brocade dresses woven with gold and silver!

Enough said. The event was reported to Don Mariano, who for the first time in his life cried with grief. And maybe he would have forgiven Mariedda, but as soon as the news spread in the Spanish battlefield, it caused such laughter and mockery at the expense of the foreign prince, that he became violently angry and wrote to his butler that he should immediately take the little Judgess with her little monster and bring them somewhere far away, to a place from which she could not return, because he was repudiating her. The butler obeyed, and one night the poor Mariedda found herself transported far from her home, in a silent and deserted countryside. In her arms, she clutched the little dog, whom she had come to love deeply.

When she was left alone in that silent and deserted countryside, in her terrible hour of despair, she finally remembered her past: she remembered Our Lady of Good Counsel and fell to the ground crying, begging for mercy and forgiveness. Then, just as it had happened in the dark and remote room of Don Juanne's house, there was a great golden light, and in it appeared the Madonna with her white dress and blue mantle, and a tiara like the Queen of Spain's.

"Mariedda, Mariedda," she said with the sweetest voice, which consoled the poor tormented girl, "you have forgotten me, and therefore misfortune befell you. But I do not abandon the afflicted, for I am the mother of those who suffer."

With her forehead to the ground, Mariedda wept and prayed.

"Mariedda," the Madonna continued, "keep walking. You will find a house that will be yours, and where you will lack for nothing. Live there until your day comes, and do not forget me again."

At that, she disappeared. The sun rose over the desolate countryside. The hedges bloomed, the streams sparkled, a sweet scent of mint wafted through the air, and a row of yellow-beaked blackbirds sang on a nearby wall. When she lifted her forehead from the ground, Mariedda found that she no longer held the little black dog. Instead, she was now holding a beautiful, rosy-cheeked little boy, whose tiny hands and feet looked like flowers. For a moment, she thought she would return to Court with that beautiful child, but then she considered the words of Our Lady of Good Counsel and immediately continued walking across the great plain that had suddenly begun blooming. She walked and walked and walked, and after many long hours she found herself in front of a beautiful green little house, hidden in a thicket of orange trees and rosebushes. From the orange trees, large golden fruit was hanging, and on the rosebushes she could see big coral flowers. Mariedda knocked, and a servant dressed in a regional costume, with a flaming-scarlet skirt, a green-gold brocade corset, and a large white veil on her head, opened the door, bowed, and asked, "Are you the mistress we were expecting?"

"Yes," Mariedda answered, smiling.

And from that day, she was in fact the mistress of that green little house hidden among orange trees and rosebushes. No one ever walked by. The world was far, far away, and yet the little house lacked for nothing: there was always golden bread, silvery water, blood-red wine, amber-colored oil, coral-like meat, honey the color of topaz, snow-white milk, and grapes that looked like bunches of pearls. There really was everything Mariedda could want, and she was happy: she prayed constantly, and waited for the promised day, when she was hoping to see her beloved husband again. Meanwhile, the beautiful little boy, whose name was Counsel, was growing like the little orange trees in the grove, and he laughed and ran on horses made of reeds, which executed swift pirouettes just for him.

Five years went by. One day, finally, a group of hunters came by the green little house: they had gotten lost in that deserted countryside and asked Mariedda for hospitality. You can imagine the pounding of Mariedda's heart, her surprise and joy, when she realized that her husband was the leader of those lost hunters! "The day has finally come!" she thought, trembling. But she did not reveal who she was, because she had changed considerably and was wearing the regional costume. Still, she graciously welcomed the hunters, among whom was Don Juanne, the devil's physician. Everyone was enchanted with the warm welcome and with Mariedda's and Counsel's beauty. At the dinner table, Don Mariano, who was sitting next to the mistress of the house, told her about his misfortune and that he had regretted the atrocious orders he had given. He said that he had searched for his poor bride across all the mountains and valleys of Sardinia, and that since he was unable to find her, he was now the unhappiest man on earth, tormented by remorse and memories. Mariedda was moved by this tale, and decided to reveal her identity before the hunters departed.

Meanwhile, something extraordinary happened, and it showed how God's justice reveals itself even in the smallest of things. Listen. A gold teaspoon from the table flatware had fallen to the floor. Counsel, who was playing among the chairs, picked it up, and—after crawling under the table—playfully placed it inside Don Juanne's embroidered leather slipper. Then, the little boy left, and the servant put him to bed. When the table was being cleared, the absence of the golden teaspoon was noticed, but no one could find it anywhere.

"Good lord," Mariedda then told the prince, "I have granted hospitality to you and to your knights. Why then do you repay me like this?"

And she told the story of the golden teaspoon that had been undoubtedly stolen by one of the hunters. Don Mariano became furious and cried, unsheathing his sword: "Knights, one of you here has stolen. Confess your shame or you will regret it bitterly!"

Everyone denied it, so Don Mariano spoke again: "Well, good lords, I will search your persons myself, and woe to the unworthy traitor who has thus repaid the hospitality of this noble lady. I will pierce him with my own sword."

Just after saying this, he searched all the hunters, and found the golden teaspoon in Don Juanne's embroidered leather slipper. In vain did Mariedda's uncle protest his innocence.

"Sir," the prince told him, "You will die by my own hand."

And he was about to kill him when Mariedda, moved to pity, asked that he be spared, and, much to the prince's delight, revealed her identity. Moved by this scene, Don Juanne threw himself at the feet of his niece, who had saved him, and confessed his sins. Mariedda and the prince forgave him, except that, as a penance, they ordered him to always remain in the green little house hidden among the orange trees and rosebushes, so that he might repent and expiate his sins in solitude. We do not know whether he did in fact repent. We do know, however, that he never left that place. Mariedda, Counsel on his reed horse, the servant in her regional costume and veil, Don Mariano, and all the other hunters returned instead to Court, where they were welcomed with great celebration, and where they lived happily for a long time. While they were passing near the ponds, that fisherman who had sung when Mariedda had first arrived in Oristano this time sang this song:

> O birds who are flying
> Flying with me
> You may now go and then come back,
> For the queen and the king are together again.

The Three Talismans

In the mountain chain surrounding the Sardinian village of Nurri, and more precisely within the mountainous area called *Pala Perdixi* or *Corongius*, there is a large and impressive natural cave, where peasants and shepherds would take refuge in order to rest and sometimes spend the night. One evening, three brothers, who were good citizens of the village and exhausted from picking olives all day, entered the cave with the intention of resting a while. Just as they were calmly discussing among themselves some business matters, while dining on bread and not much else, they saw three women come in. The women stopped and hovered at the entrance, looking at the brothers with some diffidence. But immediately the three brothers, who were nice young men, kindly invited them to come in and share their dinner. The women accepted. When the meal was over, after some small talk, the women asked the three men who they were.

"We are three orphan brothers," they answered graciously, "and we work in order to live. We are very poor, and if we knew how to improve our condition, we would certainly do it."

The three women, who were witches or fairies (known in Sardinia as *orgianas*), looked at each other for a while, and discussed something among themselves using a strange language that sounded like a cat's meow.

Then, the oldest of the three took a tablecloth out of her pocket and gave it to the oldest brother, saying: "Good man, take this gift I am giving you as a true friend. Every time you want to eat—whether alone, with your brothers, or with anyone you know—you will simply shake this tablecloth three times, and then lay it down wherever you want. All kinds of good things will appear on the tablecloth."

The second fairy turned to the second brother and offered him a wallet, saying: "You take this wallet. Every time you open it, you will find as much money as you want."

In the meantime, the youngest fairy handed a triple flute (called *sas leoneddas* in Sardinian) to the third brother, with these words: "I give you this wind instrument: it will be useful not just to you, but to anyone else who might play it and hear it. Go, dear boy, as I have nothing more than this, but you will see that this humble gift will serve you better than even the tablecloth and wallet will serve your brothers."

After this exchange, the young men and the three fairies parted amiably, thanking one another, and extending the ritual *teneis'accontu* (take care of yourselves) of southern Sardinians.

Now that they owned their marvelous talismans, the three young men no longer needed to work. So, they started to travel through the cities of Sardinia in search of adventures and pleasure.

Wherever they went, they left traces of their charity and generosity, for they were good-hearted young men. But one day a powerful—indeed, a *very* powerful—priest ordered them to stop using their talismans under penalty of excommunication and prison.

Although the legend is not clear on this point, the story (please allow me a small tangent) probably alludes to the Inquisition established in Sardinia around the middle of the fifteenth century, but practiced also before that time by some Friars Minor, and imported of course from Spain.

The three brothers laughed at the priest's orders. The talismans were invisible to all, except to their owners. Therefore, the three had nothing to fear. At the priest's repeated threats, the youngest brother started playing his triple flute, which magically made everyone who heard it dance—except for the three brothers. And then the priest, against his will, started dancing with an unstoppable energy, which made him look totally ridiculous.

Many people came over, but as they approached and heard the magical sound more clearly, they, too, started dancing and were unable to stop. Within a short time, the street was full of people who looked crazed. They all jumped around madly, twisting, begging the mysterious musician for mercy. The musician, however, was having too much fun watching the priest dance. Indeed, this priest was fat and round and suffered more than the others because of that infernal dance, and the brother did not stop playing until he saw the priest fall to the ground exhausted and unconscious.

After this episode, the three brothers ran away, but they were soon caught, tied up, and thrown to the bottom of a dungeon. Yet, even down there, they had fun playing, dancing, and eating together with the other prisoners and the prison guards.

For this reason, their trial was quickly concluded, and, after being condemned to death, they were led to the scaffold a few days later. A huge river of people, some of whom had come from distant villages, crowded all around to enjoy the spectacle of the hanging of the three sorcerers.

When they were about to die, the three prisoners asked the magistrate to grant them one last wish each. And since prisoners are never denied one last wish—with the exception of the wish for life—the three brothers obtained what they asked for.

The first asked to offer a lunch to the crowd, including the judges.

The crowd welcomed the offer with great enthusiasm, and immediately the young man lay down his tablecloth on the platform. All sorts of dishes, fruits, sweets, and fine wines appeared on this strange table. People ate and drank to their heart's desire, and yet the more they ate, the more food appeared in abundance on the table.

Within a short time, all—guards, executioners, people, and magistrates—were as drunk and full as they could possibly be. At that point, the second brother asked for the wish to distribute money. As you can well imagine, it was granted. The prisoner opened the enchanted wallet and distributed huge sums of money to those poor devils, in coins and exchange vouchers (bills did not exist yet). Soldiers, peasants, and shepherds—none of them had ever seen such a miracle before.

While everyone gave in to a crazy cheerfulness—as we ourselves would have surely done, both writer and readers, despite our seriousness and our noble contempt for money—the third brother asked, as a formality, for his wish: to play his triple flute. Hoping for another gift, the judges and the crowd boisterously granted him this last wish. Standing on the deadly platform, the young man started to play, and immediately the drunken crowds, the judges, the soldiers, and the executioners began performing a furious and macabre dance, pushing against each other, crushing and hitting each other, falling down, some fainted, some wounded, and some even dead. And in this terrible confusion, the three prisoners were able to escape and save themselves and their talismans.

The She-Mule of Abbess Sofia

I'd like you to know that a long, long time ago—over seven hundred years ago, I think—the Lord of Pratovecchio was called Count Guido of the Guidi family. His wife, Lady Emilia, had given him just a son, Ruggero, and a daughter, Sofia. Nature, however, took pleasure in giving Sofia a masculine spirit, whereas Ruggero's feminine temperament was more fitting for a woman's domestic lifestyle than for the bold feats of war. Thus, as soon as Sofia was old enough, she accompanied her father riding and hunting, with a falcon on her fist. Indeed, she enjoyed a polished armor much more than a lady's fancy necklace. Ruggero, instead, liked playing the lute and listening to the ladies of the castle gossip as they bent over their needlework.

Ruggero's inclinations brought much grief to the proud Count Guido, who feared that the heir to his name would not be able to defend the family's estate and might even lead to its ruin. Even Ruggero's physique was girlish. He was small, thin, and blond, with a pale complexion. He tired easily when handling a sword or a spear, and physical games made him uncomfortable and sick. Sofia, instead, was tall and dark-haired, ran like a deer, knew how to throw darts, and could not stay still for long within the closed rooms of Pratovecchio. She was brave and a true leader, born to govern and be feared. Naturally, since Ruggero spent more time with his mother, he knew a lot about women's genteel skills, whereas Sofia was passionate only about the things of war.

When Sofia reached a marriageable age, she rejected each and every one of the lords who came asking for her hand in marriage. Her father did not push her to wed because he would have been sad to lose her as a riding and hunting companion. In fact, she had a virile spirit and handled weapons with great skill. But as the years passed, Count Guido was becoming older and weaker.

One day, Sofia was sitting in the great hall of the palace of Pratovecchio under the roughly hewn hood of the stone fireplace, where an oak log was burning. It was the coldest season of the year, and the Count was sad, for he was beginning to feel the aches and pains of old age. He had to come to terms with the fact that upon his death there would be no one to defend the castle against the violent attacks of his enemies, because clearly Ruggero had none of the skills necessary to fight effectively. Sofia could read these anxious thoughts on her father's forehead.

So, on that day, she placed her hands on his knees, and, looking straight at him, she said: "My lord and father, unfortunately I am a woman and may not wear armor, nor act as I want to defend our lands. And speaking of self-defense, let's not even bring Ruggero into this. In my brother's hands, our lineage would surely perish. You know that I have rejected the marriage offers of many lords, not because I thought them unworthy of my hand, but because I believed that, if I left this castle, our family and our tenants would lose a capable protector. Unfortunately, dear father, human life is short, and on the day when your eyes shall close, I must be nearby so as to place my strength and my mind at the service of our family. For this reason, I ask that you build a monastery next to our castle so that I may become its abbess. Other than the lords of these castles, I know there are only bishops, abbots, and abbesses who live freely and freely lead. You know, my lord, that I was born to lead, and not to obey. If I were abbess, I could watch over my brother's estates and fulfill my need to lead, without leaving our property."

"Dear daughter, your request is granted. Tomorrow, Master Baldo, our doctor, will write a letter to the Emperor, in which I will ask that the new abbey shall rule over the nearby lands and villages. In the meantime, you need to decide what saint you wish the monastery to be dedicated to."

The old lord took Sofia's proud head in his trembling hands and kissed her on the forehead. The young woman retired to her room and took an illustrated saints' book out of an old wooden chest. She could not read, but could guess the stories of the martyrs, the saints, and their miracles from the illuminated images painted by a Camaldolese monk. Her eyes were drawn to a page depicting the bleeding head of Saint John the Evangelist, resting on a tray covered in blood. Sofia felt as if the saint's eyes were looking at her imploringly and even saw tears running down those bruised cheeks.

"That is the saint to whom I shall dedicate the new abbey!" said the young woman. "And my nuns shall follow the rule of Saint Romuald, founder of the Camaldolese order, in honor of the Camaldolese monk who painted that saint's head."

That night, Sofia dreamed only of the bloody head of Herod's victim, and saw herself dressed in the long white habit of the order, at the head of a long procession of nuns.

The next morning, she crossed the drawbridge of the castle and arrived at the spot where she wanted her new monastery built. She was followed only by two valets and her father confessor. Sofia had taken just a few steps along the castle moat when she saw a white she-mule lying on the ground, exhausted with fatigue and suffering from sores all over her back and legs. It looked as if the poor beast was about to breathe her last. But when she saw Sofia, she made one last effort and, mustering whatever strength she had left, got up suddenly and approached the young woman, neighing. Sofia tore a few blades of dry grass from the edge of the moat and offered them to the animal. Wobbling and shaking her head, the mule took them and began chewing. Still faltering on her unstable legs, the poor animal followed Sofia all the way to the place where she intended to build the monastery, and once they arrived, the mule fell suddenly to the ground.

The lady ordered one of the valets to return to the palace and fetch a stretcher with four strong men to carry the exhausted animal to the stable. The men arrived, but no matter how hard they tried, they were unable to move the mule. Then Sofia, aware that the wind was blowing icily from the mountains, and seeing that the snow was beginning to whirl, ordered the men not to bother with caring for that poor animal's agony and to build a shelter with branches so that the snow would not bury her.

Sofia's orders were immediately carried out. The she-mule was brought hay and water and covered with a blanket, and only when the young woman saw that the sick animal wanted for nothing did she return to the castle.

On that same day, Count Guido of Pratovecchio sent to Emperor Lothar a messenger with a letter in which he asked for the creation of the Abbey of Saint John the Evangelist, of the Order of Saint Romuald, as well as for the investiture of that abbey to his daughter.

The Emperor's answer took a very long time to arrive, but the wait did not seem long to Sofia because such marvelous events took place during that wait that she was kept busy day and night.

The following morning, even though snow covered the ground, Sofia left with her usual retinue to go visit the she-mule. She had barely crossed the drawbridge when the animal began to neigh with joy.

"Mother of God, this is a miracle!" exclaimed the young Corrado of Barberino, one of the valets accompanying Sofia. "The mule is alive! I would not have bet a single coin on her carcass: she looked as good as dead."

Indeed, the mule was not only alive but stood strong and healthy on her own four legs and sniffed the wind with her nostrils, as if impatient to take off running. Her sores had healed overnight, as if by magic. And now that the animal was strong and healthy, it was clear that she was not an ordinary mule but rather one of those accustomed to carrying popes, abbots, and noblewomen.

Sofia led the mule to the castle and had her placed in the stables that housed the Count's horses. She had a soft bed made for her new mount and ordered her women to quilt a beautiful caparison of crimson cloth. From that day on, Sofia rode nothing else. Indeed, the she-mule was so agile and self-assured that no horse beat her at racing, nor was any other animal better at climbing the steep mountain paths of that region.

In the meantime, construction had begun on the church and monastery dedicated to Saint John the Evangelist. Every day, Sofia went to check on the progress and to give orders, and Count Guido was even more impatient than his daughter to see the building completed quickly, because it would become the home of his beloved Sofia.

When Emperor Lothar's affirmative answer arrived, the building already had a roof, and looked more like a fortress than a monastery. All that was left to do now was to bless the church. In the

new monastery, Sofia had a beautiful stable built for her she-mule, right under her own bedroom. A hatch on the floor of her room led to the stable through a ladder so that the abbess was able to reach the mule directly and, if necessary, climb on her and run wherever need called her. This is because Sofia had not forgotten that she was supposed to defend her brother and their family possessions.

As soon as the people of the Casentino region learned that Count Guido's daughter had founded a monastery, countless young women from the local nobility requested admission, for they preferred the calm life of the cloister to the tumultuous life of the castle. On the day when the abbot came down in great pomp from the Hermitage of Camaldoli to bless the house and the convent, twenty noble young women already surrounded Sofia, along with many peasant women who were content with the humble office of lay sisters.

Count Guido and Countess Emilia wanted the most magnificent of ceremonies and regaled the church with gifts of precious ornaments, crosses, cups, lamps, candelabra, and vestments.

Just a few days after Sofia wore the white habit of the order of Saint Romuald, the old Count died in the arms of his loved ones, entrusting his daughter once more with the care of her mother, her brother Ruggero, and their tenants. There was a solemn funeral, and the Count's body was buried in the tomb of the church, under the care of the Abbess Sofia.

As soon as the old man closed his eyes, the Lord of Porciano's greed began to awaken. Everyone knew that Ruggero was weak, and in those days—when might and arrogance were the law of the land—it was thought that such an important estate as Pratovecchio should not remain in the hands of someone unable to defend it. The Count was a proud knight, and together with his four sons took up arms and descended from their lands, followed by a crowd of soldiers. Their plan was to lay siege and capture Pratovecchio, which they believed to be defenseless.

But Sofia was watching, and especially her she-mule was also watching. As soon as the lords of Porciano had come down from their castle, the mule started scraping the floor with her paws, snorting and neighing, and Sofia became suspicious, since she firmly believed that her mule had been sent to her by Saint John. Thus, even though it was the middle of the night, she ran over to the castle to prepare its defense. She placed men at every battlement and, after giving all the essential orders, returned to the monastery and rang the warning bells. The tenants who depended on the abbey came from every corner of the land. Since Sofia held within the walls of the cloister a veritable war arsenal, she armed them and ordered them to defend the place. Thus, when the lords of Porciano appeared in front of the castle ready to assault it, Sofia unfolded the banner with the quilted head of Saint John the Evangelist, climbed on her white she-mule, and went to meet them at the head of her armed men.

"Dear Count, why do you come prepared for war?" asked Sofia, stopping just a few paces from the Lord of Porciano. "What offense have I or my brother done to you?"

"I am not used to discussing war matters with women," answered the Count. "Go back to your monastery, my lady, and contemplate the things of the spirit."

"I contemplate the things of the spirit when there is no danger threatening us. Right now, however, self-defense is my only care."

A mocking laughter erupted from the troops of the men from Porciano. Sofia felt her blood boil in her veins and, after grabbing the shield and the sword offered by her young valet, Corrado of Barberino, she moved bravely toward her enemies, crying:

"By Saint John the Evangelist, follow me, my faithful ones!"

All at once, the she-mule rushed over and entered the fray. She snorted, broke through the enemy lines, and hit whatever horses stood before her with her head and with her legs. Meanwhile, Sofia's sword massacred her enemies. The white-clad woman and the white she-mule looked like a single ghost bent on nothing but destruction.

Sofia's sword flashed brightly, and after she wounded many of his men, she plunged it into the neck of the Lord of Porciano. A cry of fear immediately arose from the troops of the assailants when they saw their leader fall, and they all fled hastily into the countryside.

Waving her banner as a sign of victory, Sofia ordered her men to take the wounded enemy and bring him to the monastery, saying: "If the lords of Porciano want their leader back, they must come and fetch him at the castle."

The last of the enemy soldiers must have heard these challenging words, because two days later, after seeking reinforcements from their dependents—all minor lords from the small castles at the foot of the Apennine Mountains—they showed up stronger than the first time. Then, they sent a messenger to Sofia, declaring that they wanted to face Count Ruggero in battle directly, instead of a nun who invoked the help of Heaven . . . and perhaps even of Hell.

Sofia received the messenger, though not in the great hall of her abbey but instead in the courtyard of the castle. She had just returned from an inspection of her lands with her brother.

"Tell your master that tomorrow at dawn, the Lord of Pratovecchio will descend onto the open field, where you are to await him. He does not like to speak, but he does fight with great pleasure, and once he has unsaddled the firstborn of the lords of Porciano, he will face the secondborn, then the third, and also the fourth," replied the proud nun.

The messenger bowed, and the valets and soldiers led him back over the drawbridge. As soon as the messenger left, Sofia ran to hold up her brother, who was about to faint.

"Why?" he asked with a trembling voice. "Why did you make that promise in my name? I will never fight. I would simply die if I had to descend onto the battlefield."

"Calm down, dear lord," answered the abbess with a mocking smile. "If I have made a promise, I shall honor it, and the knight who will unsaddle the lords of Porciano will not be you, but me."

After she said this, she led Ruggero back to their mother. He was more dead than alive, and Sofia asked the Countess to watch over her son, given his wretched state.

She then distributed the weapons, assigned a place to each man, and, after going to her arsenal and choosing polished armor, a sword, a spear, a dagger, and a shield, she had her weapons brought to her room in the monastery, ordering that the doors to the castle be locked and opened only when she waved the banner with Saint John the Evangelist. From inside the monastery, Sofia prepared for war: she deployed a large number of armed men in front of the abbey and the palace, and before dawn she took to the field, wearing her armor and riding her she-mule.

The prisoner's firstborn son soon arrived. After positioning his men right in front of the men of Pratovecchio, he saluted the enemy soldier, and the duel began with the spear. Carried by her patient mount, Sofia attacked the knight within seconds: the impact of the abbess's spear on the knight, and of the she-mule on his horse, made them both fall to the ground. When his men saw this, they were blinded by anger and plunged toward Sofia immediately. Behind them, a large band of soldiers moved to their aid. The strikes fell like hail on the abbess's helmet and armor, and she could not even raise her arm to defend herself. In the meantime, however, her mule was snorting, kicking, and stomping over the body of the fallen enemy, and the Count died amid atrocious suffering.

As soon as the Count's soul left his body, the mule rose up from the ground like a bird, defeating the enemies with her kicks. She then brought Sofia to a nearby spot, where she could use her weapons against her enemies.

In addition to unsaddling the firstborn of the Lord of Porciano, the brave abbess also unsaddled the second son, and she would have easily defeated the other two, as well, had they not fled. She then took from the hands of Corrado of Barberino the banner with the head of Saint John the Evangelist and waved it as a sign of victory, inviting her men to run after the fugitives.

The enemies came back on the next day, humbly seeking peace. They asked for the body of their deceased brother, the liberation of their father, and the return of their other wounded brother. In exchange for all of this, they offered lands and a large sum of money.

Sofia was wearing her knight's uniform when she received the messenger. She agreed to his requests as long as the lords of Porciano promised never to bother the lords of Pratovecchio again. These conditions had to be put in writing, including the written admission that it would be disloyal of them not to keep their promises.

Promises cost nothing and are easily made, but it is far easier to break them than to keep them. This is exactly what happened with the lords of Porciano. As soon as they had their prisoners back, they started thinking about revenge. By now, they had found out that it was Sofia, the proud abbess, who had conquered them, and there was no way they could swallow this humiliation inflicted upon them by a woman. They could not deny, however, that Sofia was skilled with weapons, and they did not want to fight with her for fear of suffering another disgrace. Therefore, they decided to kidnap her and have her pay for her bravado with a long captivity, and perhaps even with death. Sofia herself was too honest to suppose that the lords of Porciano were planning to betray her, and she could not guess that four knights, an old man among them, would retract their own word and expose themselves to a general accusation of cowardice. Not fearing an attack, she devoted herself to the care of her monastery and to spiritual exercises. In her free time, she visited her mother and her brother, who was becoming softer and more effeminate with each passing day.

One evening, then, while Sofia was returning from the palace to her abbey thinking of the sad impression left on her when she found her brother bent over the loom, intent on weaving a silk veil as if he were a female servant, she saw a group of armed men come out of a thicket of trees. Before she even had time to scream, they tied her up, gagged her, and tossed her like a sack on the back of a horse. Then, they left, taking her with them as a prisoner.

At the abbey, people waited a long time for the abbess, but when they did not see her coming, they sent servants to look everywhere for her.

"What could have happened?" the nuns asked one another.

They went into her room and found it empty, so they went down to the stable where the she-mule was tied to the manger—but she was snorting and scratching, and her eyes were flashing brightly. Finally, the animal pulled hard on her rope, which broke. Then, she kicked open the gate to the stable, rushed into the courtyard, sprinted and leaped over the abbey walls and moats, and off she went galloping wildly toward Porciano.

When they saw the animal running off in such a furious haste, the nuns were astonished. They stopped searching for the abbess and gathered in the church before the image of Saint John the Evangelist, which they illuminated with lamps. They remained in prayer for many hours. Meanwhile, the she-mule was running toward Porciano so fast that her feet were barely touching the ground. It was night by the time the animal reached the castle, and the drawbridge, which had been lowered to let in Sofia and her kidnappers, had been raised again. The she-mule jumped up high, crossed the moat, and went through the small side gate, knocking over everyone who stood in her way. She stopped before the locked door to a cellar. The animal seemed to hear a familiar voice because she pricked up her ears, snorted, and kicked against the door to make herself heard.

Some of the armed men, frightened by the furious white beast, quickly shut themselves inside a room. The others peeked over the landing of the stairway, but they did not have the courage to come down. Meanwhile, the she-mule continued to make an infernal noise in front of the door to that cellar. Realizing that the door was impervious to her kicks, the animal was getting increasingly ferocious and took to the stairs, which she climbed quickly, and like a lightning bolt entered the great hall of the palace. Here, the young lords of Porciano were gathered around their father, laughing about their success in caging the proud abbess.

When they saw the white she-mule, the old Count and his sons let out a cry of terror and tried to take refuge in the other rooms. But the mule ran after them, pushing them against the wall. She threw them to the ground and, by kicking, biting, and pawing, killed them all.

When she saw Sofia's enemies lying on the ground like rags, the mule went down the stairway and grabbed the jailor with her teeth while he was crossing the courtyard to escape. Then, the mule dragged him in front of the door to the cellar and did not let go of him until he opened the prison door. Immediately, the mule began to neigh, and as soon as Sofia heard her, she climbed up the narrow stairway carved into the stone, jumped onto the animal's back, and arrived safe and sound to her abbey a short time after that. Once there, the abbess had the bells tolled to warn the people of Pratovecchio to take up arms—though there was in fact no need, because the people of Porciano had to bury their lords, and they were so terrified of the she-mule that they would never again dare approach the abbey or the castle.

After these events, no one disturbed Sofia's tranquil life ever again. Her mother and her brother, Ruggero, passed away placidly, and the abbess alone stayed on as the sole guardian of the castle.

She lived a long life, and the she-mule remained strong and agile for the entire time that Sofia lived in this world. In the abbey and throughout the Casentino region, the animal's long life was believed to be a miracle, and it was said that the Madonna and Saint John the Evangelist had sent Sofia that animal, as a help and support for the events of a life divided between the care of the monastery and the defense of vast estates. Indeed, on the day when Sofia passed away, the she-mule broke her halter and ran off, and no one ever saw her again.

At the abbess's death, the attacks to the castle and the abbey started up again, until Emperor Corrado, who had succeeded Lothar, gave that estate to another Count Guidi.

And here the tale ends.

Lavella's Stepmother

Once upon a time, in the city of Caprese in the Casentino region, there lived a lord from the Catani family whose first name was Beltramo and whose wife had died in giving birth to a little girl named Lavella. Beltramo buried his wife honorably, but a while after that he decided to take another wife and chose her from the Ubertini household of Arezzo. This woman was neither beautiful nor gracious, nor did she have a good character. But unfortunately, Count Beltrano only realized these things after he had already taken her into his home in Caprese, and by that point it was too late.

The first words that Lady Chiarenza said to Lavella were, "What an ugly creature!"

Fortunately, Lavella did not understand, because she was still a baby. Her nurse, however, understood all too well, and because she realized that this woman would only persecute the little girl, she never allowed Lady Chiarenza to see Lavella.

Lavella's first few years of life were quiet, because her loving nurse took good care of her. But as soon as Lavella turned seven, Chiarenza wanted to be the one to take care of her and told her husband that, if he left his daughter in the hands of a peasant, she would grow up rough and uncouth.

Chiarenza had given her husband only a daughter, who was three when Lavella turned seven. But whereas the older girl was beautiful, white as a lily, and red as a carnation, the younger one was yellow as a dried-up apple and so thin and pale that she looked more dead than alive. When Chiarenza saw the two little girls next to each other, she was overcome with a terrible envy toward her stepdaughter and never stopped tormenting her.

In order to make Lavella's face lose its pink color, Chiarenza never let her out of her rooms, forcing her to spend the entire day bent over the loom, quilting carpets and banners, or else praying on her knees on the stone slabs in the dark chapel. But even that life of seclusion could not alter the little girl's beauty. She became a little more delicate, but not any less attractive. On the contrary, it seemed that with each passing day, new charms appeared upon Lavella's features, and her heart grew in goodness and sweetness. No complaint ever left her mouth, and the pageboys and valets of the castle of Caprese called her the little angel, so celestial was the smile brightening up her face. The companions of Countess Chiarenza, on the other hand, always spoke about Lavella with contempt in order to please their mistress, and tried with every means to accuse her of being mean to her sister.

Count Beltramo heard neither the praises of the valets and pageboys nor the disparagements of the women. He spent his life either hunting or at war, and when he returned to the castle, he did not allow anyone in his presence to speak—except for Friar Uguccione, a monk, who in his youth had worn a knight's armor and had seen more battles than he had hair on his head. Father Uguccione brought joy to the Count's leisure by telling him about the court at Urbino, where he had lived, and about the court at Rimini, and about the many brave knights he met during his journeys across Italy, before he became a monk.

During those vigils, Chiarenza stayed on the other side of the room, surrounded by her ladies-in-waiting, listening to the stories with an attentive ear, but without daring to interrupt.

When Beltramo and Chiarenza retired to their quarters, the Count kept on telling his wife that he was afflicted because he did not have a son, a handsome and strong heir he could train for fighting and to whom he could hand down his name and his lands.

"Your first wife was not able to give you a son, either," the Countess replied.

"But at least Lavella is a beauty, whereas your Selvaggia is a monster I am ashamed of," replied Beltramo.

This comparison infuriated Lady Chiarenza, but in the presence of her husband and lord she was able to control herself. As soon as Lavella crossed her path, however, she made her unfortunate stepdaughter pay for all her own resentment. If, God forbid, the little girl made a mistake in the embroidery that Chiarenza assigned her, she received blows on her fingers. If she cried, Chiarenza ordered her shut inside a dark closet for hours and hours. But Lavella always kept quiet and never rebelled against her stepmother, who continuously inflicted punishments on her. It must be said, however, that each time Lavella received those blows on her fingers, she felt a sweet and invisible hand give her so many caresses that the sting went away. And when Chiarenza shut her inside that dark closet, the room lit up immediately with a glowing light, and a choir of harmonious voices sang holy hymns. Meanwhile, Lavella joined her own voice to the melodious ones and in this way time passed quickly.

As soon as the sound of approaching footsteps came near, however, the voices grew quiet, and the light disappeared. Still, Lavella's beautiful face kept that blissful expression which irritated her stepmother so much. Thus, Lavella reached her fifteenth birthday, and all those who looked at her stared with their mouths wide open, for she was so very beautiful, and the goodness of her heart was evident in her face. Although her companions never tired of telling her "Lavella is getting ugly, Lavella is becoming a monster," Chiarenza could nevertheless see that each day her stepdaughter grew in grace and beauty, and she realized that Selvaggia, instead, re-mained yellow and wrinkly as when she was little, so that, given the chance, Chiarenza would have torn her stepdaughter apart with her own hands.

Since Lavella was now fifteen years old, Count Beltramo was proud of her and wanted to take her hunting with him. Oftentimes, when he rode to the castles of Chitignano or Bibbiena, he invited Lavella to come with him in addition to being accompanied by his wife.

Because of her stepmother's stinginess and perfidy, Lavella did not own clothes appropriate for a young lady from a noble family, and although she was not in the least vain about her appearance, she came up with excuses not to join her father. But she was allowed to remain in Caprese only one out of the ten times she asked, and in the meantime the fame of her beauty extended across the Casen-tino region, and already there were songs about her, written by troubadours and spreading from mouth to mouth.

One time, Lavella was taken to a joust in Bibbiena, and the most handsome and strapping knight of the Ubertini household wore her colors when he joined the tournament. Chiarenza was biting her own hands with rage when she saw that the knight, after de-feating his opponents, went to kneel before the beautiful girl and proclaimed her the queen of the tournament.

"She will pay for this!" the stepmother told herself, seething with anger.

Shortly afterward, Beltramo left for Siena on business.

"When I return, we will celebrate the wedding," he told his wife. "Guglielmo Ubertini is in love with Lavella, all his relatives are happy with this union, and I myself could not desire a knight more brave and handsome as a successor than the winner of the tourna-ment at Bibbiena."

Chiarenza grimaced, saying that Lavella was too young to marry.

"Not at all! And anyway, I want to conclude the marriage quickly, because long things become snakes. I advise you, in fact, to take advantage of this long absence of mine to prepare the trousseau, and I will bring back gorgeous dresses for her from Siena, where they weave such beautiful cloth."

"You underestimate me," thought Chiarenza. "Lavella will never marry, and only Selvaggia's husband will inherit our castle."

Count Beltramo left with his valet and a large escort of armed men, and before climbing onto his saddle, he embraced his oldest daughter, encouraging her to stay cheerful during the time of his absence, because upon his return, he would give her some very happy news.

Lavella smiled, and for as long as she was able to see her father ride down the hills of Caprese, she waved to him with her scarf. She then returned to the room where her stepmother usually worked with her companions.

"Lavella," Chiarenza said as soon as she saw her, "now you are entrusted to me alone, and since I know how much you dislike me, I wish to spare you the annoyance of my company. Go to your room and don't leave it until your father returns."

Lavella, without saying anything, bowed her head and left. But when she was in her room, she cried and cried, holding her beautiful face between her hands. While she was so distressed, she felt a soft touch on her hair, and, lifting her eyes, she saw in front of her an angel with white wings, a white habit, and a crown of lilies on his head.

"Who are you, beautiful angel, and who has sent you to me?" asked Lavella.

"I am your guardian angel. When you were little and your mother flew up to heaven, she asked me to look after you, to cheer you up

when you were distressed, and to always protect you. Now your stepmother wants you to die before Count Beltramo's return. Consequently, you are not to accept any food from her hands, Lavella, or any from the hands of her women. The food will surely contain poison. You must eat only what I bring you, and refuse all the food that comes to you from others. The ants and the mice will come to take it away. I am the one who caressed your little hands when they were struck by blows. I am the one who called the other angels to cheer you up with their song during your long hours of imprisonment. Have trust in me."

"I trust only in you, my beautiful angel!" Lavella replied, smiling.

The angel placed a lute in her lap and disappeared. Consoled by his kind words, Lavella played some chords on the lute and started singing a sweet provençal song, accompanying the instrument with her voice.

"Listen, that nuisance is singing!" Chiarenza told her women. "Her fate will be the same as the cicada's. After singing for a month, she will die."

The women laughed at that silly joke and sought to flatter their mistress. "She will die!" they repeated. "She will die!" They did not know, however, the wicked meaning of those words, since they did not grasp Chiarenza's true intentions.

That evil woman knew the powers of certain harmful plants. She used the excuse of bringing Selvaggia out to breathe the fresh morning air so that it would seem normal for her to go into the forest. Her women could only follow her at a distance while she searched the ground for venomous plants. When she found them, she hid them among bunches of flowers. Then, after she arrived home, she crushed those herbs and mixed them into the food she sent Lavella.

But as soon as the food was brought to her, Lavella placed it on the floor and minced it for the ants and the mice, and they all brought it back to their dens. She carefully avoided eating any of it, waiting instead for her angel—who never let her go without food, and every night flew through the window of the room where Lavella was kept prisoner, bringing her berries from the forest and scented honey.

"How is Lavella?" Lady Chiarenza asked the servant who brought her food up to her every morning.

"She is white as a lily and red as a carnation," the woman replied.

Upon hearing that answer, the countess bit her hands. How was it possible that all the poison she was putting in Lavella's food had no effect on her? This is something she could not explain to herself, except if the woman to whom she entrusted her stepdaughter's food was betraying her. Therefore, she said, "I will bring Lavella's food to her myself!"

And she did bring it up to her, in fact, on that same day. However, the following morning, when she opened the room, Lavella was singing like a lark and looking better than Chiarenza herself. Furious, Chiarenza grabbed her stepdaughter by the arm and made her leave that prison, where she suspected someone entered unbeknownst to her. Pushing Lavella up a staircase, she ordered her to climb to the top. Lavella obeyed, and the Countess climbed up behind her. There were so many steps that, once she arrived at the top, her tongue was lolling out. At the top of that staircase, there was a kind of attic, without windows, closed by an iron door with three locks and three keys, all different from one another.

"Here, my dear, you will not receive any visits," Chiarenza said in a mocking tone.

And without further ado, she left, bolted the three locks, turned the three keys, and when she arrived at the bottom of the stairs, she also locked the door to the tower and went to prepare poisoned food for her stepdaughter.

Toward evening, when she climbed up the tower to bring Lavella's poisoned food to her, she heard a very sweet song coming out of the prison. Guessing a betrayal, she climbed up the steps two at a time to find out what it was. Yet, once she reached the top, out of breath, the song ceased suddenly, and there was no one in the prison but Lavella.

At that point, Chiarenza thought that perhaps her stepdaughter was a witch, but still she did not desist from offering her the poisoned food, and even obliged her to eat it in her presence. Lavella, however, remembering well the angel's recommendation, let the bread and condiments fall out of her hands as she brought them to her mouth, and the mice ran over in droves and cleaned the floor without the Countess realizing anything.

Chiarenza left the prison thinking that this time Lavella was done for, because it was not possible that all the poison she put in her food would not have a fatal effect. As she was leaving through the door, however, the angel came in through a slit in the wall and showed the girl how the more gluttonous among the mice were writhing on the floor in agony. They had eaten the food brought up by the Countess instead of carrying it to their dens.

"But what have I done to the Countess to cause her to want me dead?" the poor girl said, crying.

"Nothing, Lavella, do not cry. You will soon be consoled, and your stepmother will pay the price of so much perfidy," the angel answered her. "Get ready for a great joy," he added while listening carefully for a moment. "The horn is blowing over the hills. One of your father's valets is coming to announce his impending return. Be strong, Lavella: you only have one more ordeal to endure."

After comforting her this way, the angel disappeared, and Lavella dried her tears and kept her ears open to catch the sound of the horn, which would announce her upcoming freedom.

The tower in which the Countess kept her stepdaughter prisoner was the last one in the castle and looked toward the mountain pass. Therefore, since it was on the opposite side of the road, the sound of the horn reached it only feebly. Still, Lavella noticed that it had suddenly ceased, a sign that the drawbridge had been lowered and the first valet was already within the palace walls.

Shortly after the sound of the horn stopped, Lavella heard the noise of keys and locks and saw her stepmother enter, with her eyes popping out of her head.

Lavella got up, and her stepmother took a step back. She was frightened and ran away without turning back. She did not neglect, however, to lock the door so as to make sure that the girl would rot in that tower.

"She did not die! Surely, she is a witch," mumbled the evil woman climbing down the stairs. "But if she does not die tonight, I will be forever unable to get rid of her."

That night, Lavella, as usual, was visited by her angel, who brought her a great abundance of tasty strawberries and delicious raspberries. Before leaving, the angel gave her a small jar, advising her to loosen her hair, anoint it well with the contents of the jar, and wrap it around herself like a mantle.

After her usual prayer, Lavella restored her strength with those fresh berries and then lay down on the bare floor, taking care to wrap herself with the hair she had previously anointed with the angel's balm.

She had not yet fallen asleep when she heard a loud noise at the door. It sounded like someone was piling up bundles of sticks. But this did not frighten her, because the angel's words were still sounding in her ear, and she was hoping for her father's prompt return so that she could be freed. Lavella fell asleep full of trust, then, but after a short while, she was awakened by a loud crackling of wood. She opened her eyes and saw that her door was on fire, and that the flames were swiftly moving into her prison.

Lavella did not lose heart. She jumped up, wrapped herself in her hair, and leapt through the blaze that had been lit up right next to her prison's door. Then she ran down the stairs to escape. But at the bottom, she found the door to the tower locked, and she had to stop. From time to time, she heard a piece of the wall collapsing, and she began to think that her end was near. Suddenly, though, the door flung open, and a crowd of men rushed onto the stairway with the intention of climbing to the top of the tower. They were going to take it down so that the fire would not spread to the rest of the castle. But as soon as they saw her, they stopped in their tracks, thinking her a ghost, and she took advantage of that moment of fear to get out of their way and leave.

As soon as she was outside, she ran off, and since the drawbridge had been lowered—because the warning bells had been ringing and the locals were already arriving to help put out the fire—she fled toward the countryside and went to lie in wait in a forest, not far from the road on which Count Beltramo was bound to arrive.

At a certain point in the night, the tower collapsed with a crash, and Countess Chiarenza, who was at her window watching the fire, exclaimed: "This time that evil girl is well buried under the rubble, and Count Beltramo will be unable to find her. I will tell him that she escaped, and no one will be able to contradict me."

The evil Countess, who had kept vigil all night waiting for the tower to collapse, went to bed. However, remorse prevented her from sleeping, and at dawn she was already up with her ladies in waiting, who began dressing her. At the same time, she told them that Lavella had set fire to the tower and had run away. They pretended to believe her story, and in order to flatter her, they said that Lavella was bound to end up this way because she was disobedient, proud, and scornful.

The sounds of the horn rising from the valley made Chiarenza turn pale. Nevertheless, she took heart, got dressed, and moved toward her husband, holding Selvaggia's hand.

Lady Chiarenza waited for the Count in the Great Hall, and when she saw him appear, she went to embrace him. He pushed her away, however, and with a stern look asked her, "Where is my daughter?"

"Here she is!" replied the evil woman, pushing Selvaggia into his arms.

"I do not mean this one," said the Count. "I mean Lavella, so sweet, good, and beautiful."

"Alas, my lord! That disobedient girl gave me much grief in your absence. So, in order to return her to you the way you gave her to me, I thought it wise to keep her locked up in the tower. But I was unable to guard her even there, because she set fire to it and ran away."

"My lady, you are an evil one," said the Count. "What did you do to Lavella? If that poor girl has died because of you, you too shall die."

"I could do nothing more than lock her up, and I call Heaven as witness to my intentions!"

"Do not blaspheme!" the Count yelled, and moving to the door, he gestured toward it.

All at once, Lavella appeared. She was pale, her hair was undone, and her clothes burned. The Countess screamed when she saw her, but composed herself right away and said: "See, what I said is true. First, she set fire to the tower, and then she ran away."

"No, I am not the one who set the fire. She did, for she wanted me dead," Lavella told her father calmly. Then, turning to her stepmother, she continued: "The Lord, the Blessed Virgin, and my guardian angel saved me from the poison that you put in my food, and from the fire. What have I done to you, my lady, to deserve your hatred?"

"Listen, my lord, to her brazen accusations. Make her stop," said Chiarenza.

Lavella, struck by those words, lowered her eyes and said nothing, and Count Beltramo did not know whether to believe Lavella's stories about the cruelty she endured, or the accusations that his wife had leveled against her. But then Selvaggia, who had gone out for a moment, came back in the room holding a slice of cake, into which she was greedily sinking her teeth.

Chiarenza leaped over to her, tore the cake out of her hand, and then, opening her mouth and overwhelmed by fear, she screamed: "Spit it out! Spit it out! It's poison!"

"This is the food you used to prepare for Lavella. Dare you deny your crime?" asked the Count.

Chiarenza did not hear him. Kneeling next to her daughter, she looked at her anxiously and pushed her fingers down her throat to make her throw up the poisoned cake. But Selvaggia's face had already turned from yellow to livid.

"Help! Save her!" screamed the Countess.

Father Uguccione ran over and immediately gave the girl some medicine, but Selvaggia, instead of coming to, writhed like the mice in Lavella's prison, and screamed as if someone were killing her.

Chiarenza's stepdaughter stood on the side, looking in terror at a scene in which she recognized God's justice.

Selvaggia died in atrocious pain as her mother held her in her arms, attempting to bring her back to life with her own breath.

The Count tried to drag his wife away, but Lavella, looking at him with compassion, said: "Don't you think that she has been punished enough for her wickedness?"

"You are right," answered the Count. "Let us leave her to her pain and to her remorse. And you, daughter, go and make yourself beautiful, because soon the handsome knight Guglielmo of the Ubertini will arrive. He is the one who wore your colors at the joust in Bibbiena, and he wants to ask you to marry him."

Lavella left, and those same women who had showed her such hatred when Chiarenza had tortured her, now eagerly surrounded her, competing to get her ready and proclaim her beautiful.

The wedding took place on that same day with much pomp, and Lavella heard around herself a chorus of celestial voices that no one else could hear.

The Countess Chiarenza lay her daughter in her coffin, and while the hall resounded with cheerful sounds and pleasant conversation, she was alone in attending her daughter's funeral.

The next day, Lady Chiarenza left by order of her husband and went to live in a convent in Arezzo, while Lavella, happy daughter and wife, remained the lady of the castle.

The story does not tell about Chiarenza's end, but it is known that Lavella always remained good and beautiful, and lived a long life with her husband, to whom she gave a large number of children.

The Madonna's Veil

Many, many years ago, Count Guidi from Poppi had a sister who, after getting married in Florence, returned unexpectedly to her brother's house, without an escort, on foot, exhausted, and in tatters.

Her name was Ginevra, and she carried in her arms a baby girl only a few months old, wrapped in a light blue veil.

As soon as she arrived in the castle courtyard, Lady Ginevra collapsed with exhaustion, and the potions she was given allowed her to regain just enough strength to say: "I entrust you with my daughter. You must never take the Madonna's blue veil off her."

After making this effort to speak, Ginevra fell down dead, and her tiny child, pale and thin, was welcomed by her uncle, who brought her to his wife.

The Count of Poppi did not know how to explain the miserable life of his sister, whom he had married off three years earlier to a wealthy and powerful nobleman, Lord Buonaccorso Rucellai. To find out the cause of her misfortune, he sent messenger after messenger to Florence, but no one was able to tell him anything significant. All of them, however, assured him that Buonaccorso led a magnificent life in his palace at Via della Vigna, and that he wore mourning clothes and told everyone that his wife had died.

At that time, the Guidis were at war with the Florentine Republic, and the Count was busy defending his lands and unable to discover the truth through a private investigation. It would have been impossible for him to go to Florence without falling into enemy hands. Therefore, he was content to lay his sister's body in the family tomb, and to care for little Lisa, who was as beautiful as an angel and was beloved by everyone because she was kind and sweet.

Many years passed this way, and as Lisa grew, so did the blue veil that enveloped her from head to foot. The strange thing was that this thin cloth did not wear out with use, nor did it ever fade. On the contrary, the more Lisa wore it, the newer it looked.

Everyone who lived in Poppi noticed this fact, and as a result, the little girl was honored and revered. No one doubted that she was the Madonna's protégée, and that her veil had the virtue of healing the possessed, the mad, and all who were sick with diseases that doctors were unable to cure. People flocked to her in droves from the farthest reaches of the Casentino region, and as soon as Lisa touched the sick with that veil, reciting prayers that no one had taught her, they were fully healed. Nor was her power limited to this, since as soon as the Count's lands were burned by drought or if persistent rains threatened to make the rivers overflow, all Lisa had to do was raise her veil to the Heavens, accompanying that gesture with her usual prayers for the rains to fall, or for the sun to shine again in a cloudless sky.

The Count and his wife, aware of all the benefits they owed their niece, surrounded her with every possible care and waited anxiously for the moment when their eldest son was all grown up so that the two could marry.

One day, when Lisa was fifteen years old, the Count of Poppi was warned that a suspicious-looking stranger was arrested while mysteriously searching for something around the castle. The Count wanted to meet the stranger immediately. Yet, despite interrogating and threatening him with torture and punishment, he could not obtain any information from him.

"Fine, then, shut him in prison, and perhaps fasting will loosen his tongue," the Count said.

The order was carried out right away, but when, two days later, the guards went to take the prisoner out of the jail that was carved in the rock and had only one exit, they found him strong and robust and as stubborn as before.

The Lord of Poppi was once again unable to get the prisoner to utter a single word.

"Well," he said, "when he was arrested, this rascal probably had food stuffed in his pockets. Search him now, and if you find anything, take it away. Perhaps, after two days of fasting, he will speak."

The stranger did not offer any resistance, but in his pockets they found nothing—not even the tiniest morsel of bread. The guards started thinking that he had the power to live without food. Indeed, when he was taken out of prison two days later, he was as healthy and strong as before, and not even then was the Count of Poppi able to get him to say a single word.

"Call Lisa," he ordered in a low voice to a valet. "There must be a spell at work here."

And it is true that, as soon as Lisa appeared, wrapped from head to foot in her blue veil, smoke started coming out of the chained man's mouth and eyes. After that, he immediately disappeared without a trace.

"My child," exclaimed the Count, who enjoyed calling Lisa his daughter, "I believe that man to be the Devil himself! But what did he want?" added the lord, worried by that mystery.

Lisa fell to her knees and started praying, raising her veil to the sky. No one dared say a word as long as she remained in that pleading position, and when she got up again, she turned to her uncle and said: "My lord, only to you may I reveal the mystery that was just shared with me. Please have this room cleared."

Everyone left, and Lisa continued: "When my mother entered the Rucellai household, my father experienced a reversal of fortune. Three ships that were bringing his merchandise to the Orient sank. He entrusted the better part of his money to a Venetian merchant, who ran off with it. So, he was suddenly on the brink of having to sell his palace, since he had nothing left.

One night, overtaken by despair, and knowing that my mother was about to give him an heir, he said, 'If Satan were to ask me, I would give him the life and the soul of the child about to be born.' At this impious offer, my father's room trembled, and the roof was torn open. One moment later, Lord Buonaccorso saw the Devil in front of him, who said, 'Keep your promise and you will be saved.'

My father did not withdraw his offer. On the contrary: he wrote his infernal pact in blood on an ivory tablet. A short while later, my mother gave birth to me, and the Devil appeared in her room, ready to take me away. As my father grabbed me and was about to turn me over to the Devil, my mother tore the blue veil off a wooden statue of the Madonna next to her bed and tossed it over me. The Devil disappeared, but my father, enraged against his wife, shut her in a dungeon. However, he did not have the heart to separate me from my mother, who had promised me to the Madonna. Nevertheless, the Devil hoped to get me back and did not abandon my father. My poor mother, after almost one year of being shut in the dungeon, was freed by an old servant, who took pity on her and gave her a little money. Fearing she might be discovered, the wretched woman stayed hidden inside a cave for a long time, until she felt close to death. It was then that she decided to come here to you, so as not to leave me alone in the world. The stranger whom you kept prisoner was the Devil, who has not given up yet and will continue to lay traps for me. He was hoping to enter the castle and take off this veil that protects me."

"But who has told you all of these things?" asked the Count.

"While I was praying, I had a very clear vision of these events. I saw the unraveling of the entire painful story in a series of pictures, and above these pictures I could always see the Madonna's sweet face, smiling at me, as if promising me protection."

Lisa became silent, and the Count told no one of what he had learned. But rumors of the miracle spread throughout the county, and people were rushing over to Poppi in droves to request Lisa's help in their sickness, or even just to kiss her miraculous veil.

One Sunday, while the girl was coming home from Mass, she found a man covered from head to foot with sores lying under the arch of the castle. He was accompanied by two peasants, who had brought him up there on a cart full of straw. The man begged her to touch him with her veil so as to free him from the torments he was suffering.

The Countess and Count of Poppi hastened their step so as not to look at that revolting man, and the valets and pageboys followed their masters. Lisa was left alone in front of the sick man and his companions. As she was bending toward the wounded body to lay her veil on his sores, she felt the veil being torn off her back. The false sick man stood up, and, after taking Lisa in his arms, flew off with her, while his two companions fell into a hole that had suddenly opened in the ground. The veil was left abandoned on the ground.

After waiting for Lisa for a while, the Count and Countess sent for her, but the valets could not bring back anything more than the torn veil and the news that the sick man and his companions had disappeared. The Countess burst into tears. The Count ordered his horses to be saddled and left with a large band of men, ordering them to spread out all over the roads and search everywhere for his beloved niece.

The latter, however, was flying across space tightly held in the grips of a winged Demon, who set her down in a cave near the Tuscan Alp of Catenaia. As soon as he put her down, however, Lisa realized that a tiny bit of the miraculous veil was still stuck to her

hair, and, encouraged by this, she started praying to the Madonna fervently.

In the meantime, the veil stretched out so as to cover her entirely. As soon as she felt protected by that miraculous cloth woven by angels, she no longer feared the Devil, who was watching her intently, and walked bravely to the entrance of the cave, which was blocked by a boulder. As soon as she touched the stone with her veil, the stone rolled far away, and she was able to exit freely, while the Devil was nailed down to the ground.

Lisa did not know the area, and she wandered over the mountain all night, stopping once in a while to address a warm prayer to her Protectress. She prayed with all her heart, not only for the grace to return to the hospitable castle of Poppi, but also to beg the Heavens to free her father from his slavery to the Devil.

At daybreak, she saw the great tower of Poppi, lit by the rising sun, and began to walk faster. Finally, as she reached the plain, she met some of the Count's men. They had been looking for her all night and cried with joy when they saw her safe and sound. She climbed on a horse, and you can't even begin to imagine the welcome she received from the Count and Countess and with how much devotion they all sang the *Te Deum* hymn of praise and thanksgiving for the young woman's liberation.

The Count and Countess no longer allowed her to leave the walls of the castle, and asked her to fix the date of her marriage to their only son, so that her husband could protect her day and night from the Devil's snares. Lisa, stunned by so much honor and goodness, decided that the wedding would take place four weeks later, but added that before accepting the young Count's hand, she had a mission to accomplish: to try with all her might to save her father, whom she wanted present at her wedding.

The Count immediately sent his men to Florence to invite Messer Buonaccorso to his daughter's wedding, but when they arrived, they found him dead. When Lisa heard the news, she wept bitterly, but did not stop praying for him. One night, however, the Madonna appeared to her and said: "Beloved daughter, your prayers are useless: your father is among the damned. He was unable to free himself from the torments the Devil inflicted on him when he tried to prevent the Devil from owning you body and soul. So, he took his own life and is now in Hell among the sinners."

Realizing that she could no longer do anything for her father, Lisa prayed for the family that had welcomed her, and she called for the family to be blessed by Heaven. Soon thereafter, the wedding was celebrated, and for many long years the Countess of Poppi was the angel of the household.

■ Cordelia (Virginia Tedeschi Treves)

Fiery Eyes

When the Queen of Portugal gave birth to a beautiful princess, the Prickly Fairy present at the baptism looked at the girl and said: "Here is a nice little morsel for the Bear King."

Those impenetrable words caused the queen to fall into a deep depression. She constantly heard them echo in her ears and could not find peace. One day, therefore, she decided to consult the Nymph of the Wood, who was considered to be very powerful. The queen set out with her most trusted companion, and it took them seven months, seven days, and seven hours before they could find the Nymph of the Wood, who lived in the middle of the biggest forest on earth. Had there not been cows, deer, and other animals to show them the way, the queen and her companion would have wasted all their time and effort.

Finally, a donkey, who was smarter than some people, started braying "Hee-haw . . . Hee-haw . . ." and pointed with his pricked-up ears toward a cave. The queen understood the donkey's braying to mean "It is there, it is there," but she could not believe that a fairy as powerful as the Nymph of the Wood would live in such a cave. As soon as she entered it, however, she found a magnificent palace that shone as brightly as if it were made of diamonds, and the Nymph of the Wood was sitting on a sparkling throne surrounded by nymphs whose eyes looked like burning coals. The queen was dazzled, swooned, and fell to the ground. As if in a dream, she heard the Nymph of the Wood tell her: "I know, you came to seek my help for your daughter, whom an evil fairy has given to the Bear King, the cruelest monarch on this earth. There is a way of saving her, but you have to follow my instructions to the letter. As soon as you leave my kingdom, you shall take the princess by the hand and lead her to one of my woods. After wandering for seven days with her, she will fall asleep on a hill— at which point, you will go home and leave her to her fate. Fear not, I will always watch over her, and if she succeeds in falling in love with one of the kings or princes that I will send on her path before she turns twenty, she will be saved, and will return to your kingdom a happy bride."

"Please arrange everything so that she finds a husband before she turns twenty," the queen replied.

"I will give her fiery eyes with which she may charm all those who look at her. Nevertheless, the fairy, who is her enemy, gave her a heart of stone, which will remain hardened until she turns twenty. Then the Bear King will come to take her away. We can only hope that, among the princes I will send to her, there will be one so powerful as to offset all of the Prickly Fairy's spells and allow the princess's heart to soften before the preordained time."

Upon awakening, the queen found herself in her royal palace, as if she had never left. Although her heart ached at the thought of abandoning her daughter, still she felt impelled by an unknown force to do what the Nymph of the Wood had asked.

The queen went into the princess's room and was surprised to see that the princess's eyes shone like twin stars, and she understood that the Nymph had kept her word.

She took her daughter by the hand and led her out of the palace.

"Where are we going?" asked the princess.

"To the country," answered the queen.

The princess started running, happy as a little bird that had been freed after being kept prisoner in a cage for too long.

The queen's eyes filled with tears at the thought of abandoning her little girl.

Seven days later, the princess, who had wandered and danced that entire time while picking flowers, fell asleep on a pile of grass, and the queen felt herself drawn by an irresistible force back toward her royal palace.

When the little girl awoke, she looked around and called for her mother. Only the mountain echo answered. For a full day, she wandered around the woods looking for her mother, but when night fell, she became afraid and started crying.

A shepherd who happened to be nearby took pity on the abandoned girl and welcomed her into his hut, which was not far. The shepherd's hut was in a nice green meadow surrounded by other huts, where the cows, sheep, and the other animals he took care of slept.

He had the girl sit down and gave her a bowl of milk and some bread, which she found delicious given how hungry she was. Then he asked her if she wanted to stay with him and guard the herds. He was charmed by the girl's shining eyes, which lit up the hut with their splendor, and was hoping that she would remain with him forever to comfort his old age. She replied that she would accept his proposal but only until her mother came and found her, and in this way, she became the guardian of Gianni's cows—for that was the shepherd's name.

She lived happily and enjoyed the cows that she took to pasture, gathering flowers and making garlands with them. In the midst of her innocent fun and games, she completely forgot the queen her mother and the royal palace where she was born.

Because of her eyes, which shone like stars, everyone called her "Little Star," and she believed she had always been "Little Star."

When she turned fifteen, a handsome knight passed by those mountains, and when he saw her, he did not want to continue on his journey, for he could not take his eyes off her face.

"What do you want from me, staring at my face like that?" Little Star asked.

"I want to marry you," the youth answered.

"You are not for me," said Little Star, and ran off.

The handsome knight followed her over mountains and valleys, but she ran like the wind, and he kept on after her, saying: "I am the king's son! Stop! I want to marry you."

But she paid him no heed and ran even faster.

As he followed her, the young man tripped on a tree trunk and fell. He then woke as if from a dream, forgot all about the beautiful girl, and returned to his own country.

A year went by, and the king came hunting on those mountains, accompanied by a large retinue of knights.

Little Star wanted to see him go by, but as soon as she appeared in the middle of the main road with her fiery eyes, the king and his retinue stopped in their tracks, and as they all stood admiring her, they fell into ecstasy.

Annoyed by their gaze, she decided to return home, but the hunters followed her over woods and mountains, no longer caring about the wild animals they were supposed to be hunting.

"Go away," said Little Star.

But the men followed her and stayed on her trail.

She ran and ran, and the king followed her closely.

"I want to marry you," he said.

"I am not for you," Little Star answered.

"If you don't marry me, I will kill you," said the king, angered by her rejection.

Little Star turned around, looked him in the face, and the king was left immobile and petrified like a statue.

"He is dead," said the men of the retinue, and they moved to put Little Star in jail, but they did not dare touch her. So, while they were trying to make the king revive, the girl was able to return with old Gianni to their hut.

"You will suffer many sorrows," the old man said to her, "if you don't finally decide to marry."

"If you only knew how many times I also begged her to listen to me," said a young shepherd. "Her heart is as hard as the stones of these mountains."

"I cannot marry," said Little Star. "Our friend is right: I have a heart of stone."

In the meantime, the king's companions had discovered her dwelling and wanted to arrest her. But once they arrived in her presence, they looked into her shining eyes and fell to the ground swooning, just like their king.

The royal prince had stayed behind in his palace, but when he learned the news of what had happened, he called his trusty pageboy—a clairvoyant child, who had received a miracle-working talisman from a fairy, and told him: "You who know everything, tell me what happened to my father the king and to his retinue."

The pageboy looked into a mirror and said: "The king and his retinue are asleep in the woods, charmed by the eyes of a beautiful girl."

"I want to see this girl."

"What if you then also fall asleep?"

"You will not allow it."

"And how can I prevent it?"

"You are omnipotent, dear little pageboy. Let's go."

The pageboy, happy and proud of his master's praises, said: "We may be able to save the king and his retinue, but you will have to marry the beautiful girl."

"I will only marry a girl with royal blood."

"We shall see. Meanwhile, here is my stick. It possesses a virtue that will help you in any circumstance."

"Why are you not coming with me?" said the prince.

"I can't. I am forbidden from entering that wood."

The prince set out, melancholy and alone.

He walked all day without finding a place to rest, and he trembled as he saw night descending while he was still in that dark, thick wood. Then, he realized that there was a head with two shining eyes on the stick the pageboy had given him, and it illuminated the way. He could hear voices coming out of the vegetation, saying:

> *Ahead, far ahead*
> *You shall find the knights.*
> *If you go to the mountains*
> *The king you shall find again.*

So, he went ahead, right where those voices were leading him.

And indeed, once he reached the top of a mountain, he tripped on some object that blocked his way and lowered his gaze to look. It was a man from the king's retinue, lying on the ground as if dead.

With his stick, he hit him gently, and the man immediately woke up.

He did the same with the others he met along the way, and finally with the king, whom he found on top of the mountain. Once awake, they all wished to leave, but the prince wanted to see the beautiful girl, and as much as the king advised him against it, the prince refused to go back to the royal palace without seeing her.

Little Star was in a meadow, in the company of old Gianni, minding the cows, which were grazing quietly. When the prince arrived, she looked at him with her shining eyes, but he lifted the stick and she was dazzled, and immediately felt obliged by an irresistible force to follow the prince.

"Prince, handsome prince, do you want to marry me?" she said.

"No, because you are not of royal blood."

"But I am indeed of royal blood."

"Why are you minding the cows then?"

"It was a punishment, but you should know that last night I dreamed I am of royal blood."

She felt her heart of stone come to life, and sensed within herself a great love for the prince.

In the meantime, they had left the wood. The prince was running, and she followed him until they met the pageboy, who told the prince: "Why are you running away?"

"Because she wants to marry me."

"Marry her, then."

"But she is a peasant."

"No, she is the daughter of the King of Portugal."

The prince turned around, looked her in the face, saw the light in her eyes, and said: "Clearly, you can only be of royal blood with those dazzling eyes. Well then, I shall marry you."

As soon as he said these words, the spell was broken, and Little Star was saved. The Nymph of the Wood told the Queen of Portugal about the magic, and she came with her entire retinue to meet her daughter and her liberator, while the Bear King, vexed and angry, escaped into the enchanted wood, never to leave it again. The Nymph of the Wood had won, and Little Star, the most beautiful princess on earth, became the happy bride of Prince Valorous.

Prince Valorous's Doll

The Kingdom of the Rising Sun sank deep in mourning. No longer could one hear the customary cheerful celebrations or hymns of joy. Instead, there was squalor everywhere, and the sound of weeping. The good Queen of the Rising Sun had died, and the beautiful Princess Acacia Blossom, a lovely fifteen-year-old, had followed her mother into the grave. The King of the Rising Sun was grief-stricken. He could not accept this double misfortune, and his one hope lay in Prince Valorous, his only heir. Even on that front, however, he had nothing to be happy about.

After his sister's death, the prince had become so sad that he seemed to be losing his mind. He haunted the halls of the palace with a gloomy face, his gaze fixed on a single point, his gait as tired as an old man's. He no longer went out for walks and no longer cared about his beloved horses. He neglected hunting and his favorite games, and spent almost the entire day shut inside Acacia Blossom's room, which had remained exactly the way the princess had left it before dying.

The king was worried by his son's sadness and wondered what he might be doing all day shut inside his sister's room. So, he ordered one of his faithful servants to look at the prince's behavior through the keyhole and to report back to him. The messenger, after going to his observation spot, returned saying that the prince embraced Acacia Blossom's doll, which the princess had left on the couch.

"That does not seem possible," said the king. "You must not have seen well. Go back and try to take a better look."

The messenger obeyed, but he soon returned to the king's presence in a state of confusion, and said: "Sire, unfortunately I was not wrong: the prince is in love with Acacia Blossom's doll. He calls her by the sweetest and most loving of names and says that he wants to marry her."

"A doll!" exclaimed the king, deeply hurt by that account. "Then, the prince is mad! I cannot believe it. I must see it with my own eyes."

That said, he got up in haste and, once he reached the threshold of the princess's room, he rapped on the door. The door opened, and he walked right in, so as to surprise his son.

The prince stood in the middle of the room, holding a beautiful doll in his arms. It had blond hair and a pair of expressive eyes that sparkled and moved like real ones. He was cradling the doll tenderly, using the sweetest terms of endearment. He called the doll Stella, or Star—the same name that Acacia Blossom had also given her—and he kissed her and caressed her as one would a living being.

"What are you doing?" the king asked him in an irritated voice. "Do you think it right for a prince named Valorous to waste his days playing with dolls? Are you perhaps a little girl? Come on, let's go! Leave those childish games to others. Get on your battle horse, for he is getting bored with doing nothing, and then go, run across the open countryside to renew your burdened spirit and to strengthen your exhausted limbs."

The prince looked at his father with dreamy eyes, hesitated for a little while, then said: "But don't you know that this is my only consolation since Acacia Blossom's death? Can't you see how this doll looks at me with loving eyes? She will be my bride."

"A wooden bride! You are delirious," said the king. "Look at the doll carefully: is that the queen you want to give your people? Come on, return to your senses. Don't give me this new sorrow."

"But this doll is alive! She is alive!" exclaimed the prince, holding the doll to his heart. "Look at her smiling mouth, feel the softness of her hair. Don't tell me she is made of wood, please do not give me this new sorrow."

The king left that room shaking his head, sad and discouraged. There was no longer any doubt: his son, his only comfort, had gone crazy. Not knowing how to remedy such a disgrace, the king shut himself in his room for several hours, alone, to better reflect on his sad situation. Finally, he decided to call the sages of the land and ask for their counsel.

They came from every corner of the land, the old sages. When they were introduced to the king, they knelt humbly, offering him their services. The king told them of Prince Valorous's madness and waited to hear their verdict. They shook their heads, made some esoteric gestures, and then began to discuss and argue. Some advised one thing, some another. It really looked as if they wouldn't be able to come to an agreement. Finally, the youngest one, called Goldenbeard from the color of his beard, declared: "The only remedy is to send the prince away from these places that remind him of his adored sister. He must go and travel to unknown and faraway lands, so that the new and cheerful images he will see may rub out those painful memories."

"I am willing to send him to the end of the world," said the king, "as long as he returns to me healed."

"But will he agree to leave?" asked the old sages.

"We shall see," replied the king, and immediately had his son summoned.

When the prince arrived in the presence of the sages, the king told him: "I have been thinking about your future and consulted the sages of the kingdom so as to give you an education worthy of the heir to the throne of the Rising Sun. They advised me to send you on a journey so that you may get to know the world and succeed me in reigning with wisdom over your people. Therefore, I have chosen Goldenbeard as your traveling companion, for he is the youngest of the sages. He will guide you across foreign lands, where you shall find the vestiges of centuries past and where you will be among new people, where the progress of science will astound you."

The prince replied: "May the advice of the sages be followed, and may the will of my father the king be done."

"Now you must prepare without delay for your departure," added the king, "for once a decision has been made, it is best not to waste time in idle chatter, but instead implement it right away."

The prince bowed and left to get ready for his trip. The king thought his son would proudly oppose the idea of going far away, and so he was surprised to see him so docile and obedient, and he became more hopeful about the likelihood of his son's healing. But he was profoundly disturbed when he was told that the prince was busy having an elegant case made for his doll, lined with satin and covered in velvet with gold handles, so that he could bring it along.

This was something his father was tempted to forbid. Goldenbeard reassured him, however, and said that opposing such an innocent desire was useless, for the king could be certain that, after a few days of travel, the doll would lie forgotten in the velvet case, and different thoughts would occupy the prince. The king put his trust in the wise man's words, and commended his son to him, saying: "Remember to bring him back to me healed. I would give half my kingdom to see him happy and carefree as he once was." Then he climbed atop the highest tower of the palace, where he could see the ship with its blue sails waiting, rocking gently on the waves.

The prince refused to climb aboard the ship until he saw that the case carrying his treasure was well settled. He then sat next to the case without losing sight of it for a single moment. He did not care about the blue sea, nor about the landscape before his gaze. He only thought about his doll. And when a stormy wind was by turns lifting the ship toward the sky and then threatening to submerge it into the deep abyss, he did not fear for his life, but held on tight to the case, fearing that the wind might toss it into the sea, or else that the Captain might want to throw it overboard to remove the extra weight from the ship.

Goldenbeard never took his gaze off the prince, as if he were hypnotizing him. The sage stood like a wizard at the center of the ship amid the fury of the storm, and appeared to be the master of the sea and of the elements.

"Make the storm stop, you who are wise," the prince kept asking him.

"Fear not, soon we will arrive at port," Goldenbeard answered.

There was talk already of tossing every useless weight into the sea, and the prince feared for his case.

"Make the storm stop, you who are powerful," he repeatedly begged Goldenbeard.

"My power has no effect against the fury of the elements, but my gaze sees far, and already the colors of the rainbow are appearing on the horizon. Take heart, my prince, and your precious cargo will be safe, I promise you." And while he said this, he laid his arms alternately on the case, as if to protect it, and on the sea, as if to calm its fury.

Indeed, within a few moments, the whirling waves subsided. A rainbow appeared across the sky, and the ship passed through its colorful semicircle as if under a triumphal arch. It was sunset, and in the distance, one could see land and the white houses that crowned the sea, forming a gulf. Their little lights looked like beaming stars, inviting sailors to rest. Prince Valorous was glad they would soon be landing, and he would be able to lay his precious case in a safe place.

As soon as they arrived at a little house on the seashore, the prince begged Goldenbeard to let him take the case up to his room. Once there, his first care was to open it and take out the doll, hold her in his arms, and rock and caress her. He then placed her sitting in an armchair, as if on a throne. He kneeled before her, expressed his love for her, and called her his Stella. Then he begged her forgiveness for shutting her so long in her case, as in a tomb.

Goldenbeard let him vent his affections, then told him: "Remember who you are, and the purpose of your journey. As the king your father told you, it is not worthy of a Valorous prince to shut himself in the house and adore a doll: you are a prince, not a weak little girl."

"Acacia Blossom's soul is in this doll! Can't you see how she smiles? I had to compensate her for keeping her shut in for so long," replied the prince.

"Your sister was wise and brave, and, if she were here right now, she would surely push you to travel the world, and to acquire knowledge and experience so that you can reign wisely over your people. Look," added Goldenbeard, pointing to the landscape out the window. "If the spectacle of nature smiling at you and inviting you does not tempt you, we must admit that your head is as wooden as that of the doll you so admire."

The prince, sensitive to this reproach, got up suddenly, approached the balcony, and when he saw the spectacle before his eyes, forgot all about the doll, Acacia Blossom, and almost forgot as well the Kingdom of the Rising Sun. The sky had cleared after the storm, and the moon rose like a silver arc on the horizon. On the right, a crown of tiny lights surrounded gardens and homes, like a diamond necklace. On the left, linked to the land by a majestic bridge, rose an island, and in its midst was a tall mountain cut through by wide roads that snaked up to the top, where one could see a palace lit by myriads of colorful lights. From that palace came sounds, songs, and joyful voices that spread through the air in a choir of sweet melodies.

That enchanted palace was fascinating, and beckoned every desire as if through the power of a magnetic fluid. A crowd of people climbed up the difficult and steep road, eager to reach their destination. There were throngs of men and women, coaches, horses, racing cars, flying wheels, and all seemed in a frenzy to climb up quickly, as if impelled by a force more powerful than their own will.

Prince Valorous stood ecstatic before that spectacle and, forgetting his doll, asked Goldenbeard: "Where are all those people going? What is the name of that palace?"

"It is the Palace of Illusions," answered the sage. "Everyone is attracted by its light, and so they run and run, fearing that the arrival of dawn may cause the disappearance of the enchanted castle."

"Let us also go there too, then, right away! I too want to hasten there, and see the palace," said the prince.

"What about Stella?"

"Stella can wait. You said it yourself, wise Goldenbeard, that I cannot stay here shut in like a little girl. I must see, I must learn. Let's go, then. Let's go now."

As he was saying this, the prince left the house, followed by Goldenbeard. He started toward the bridge, where a river of people flowed from every country in the world. Impelled by an irresistible force, he crossed the bridge, arrived at the foot of the mountain road, and entered it without hesitation, despite the continuous obstacles he found on his way. At every turn, he saw a warning, written with words of fire, such as:

> You rush to the light
> Like many butterflies
> But instead you will be disappointed
> When the dawn rises.

Farther ahead he saw some wise sayings:

> Not all that shines is precious.

> A ray of sun is like the foam of the sea
> Hold them tight in your hand until they both disappear.

"Did you read that?" said Goldenbeard. "We had better go back."

But the prince paid no attention to him, and forged ahead up the steep and increasingly arduous path. Goldenbeard pretended to disapprove of that adventure, but in his heart, he was happy to see that the doll was being neglected.

Meanwhile, the Palace of Illusions got closer, and it was unimaginably splendid. Its walls were made of cut diamonds refracting the thousands of lights surrounding them and forming all the colors of the rainbow. It was a dazzling spectacle. The door was made of gold and covered with gems. It was open, and, instead of valets, on either side there was a row of beautiful, smiling fairies, who with precious gestures invited people to enter their kingdom.

When the prince and Goldenbeard arrived at the threshold, they stopped because they were confused by that sea of lights. But the fairies smiled at them, and the two men were transported inside that palace of enchantments. They were in an immense round hall forming the center of a gigantic star. From this center, twelve rays fanned out, each of which led visitors to the discovery of new marvels and unseen prodigies. The center of the star was its most lively point, with fairies more beautiful than the ones who invited passersby at the entrance door. They were weightless, wearing clothes made of air and veils as impalpable as clouds, displaying all the colors visible in a summer sunset sky. There were fairies clothed in sky blue and sea green, and fairies wearing the color of opals and of oranges. Some were dressed in carmine pink, others in violet in all of its softest hues. Their heads looked like flowers on a thin stem, rocked by a spring breeze.

Prince Valorous stopped in the center of the hall, uncertain about which ray he should follow. Each one held an unusual attraction for him. In one, precious stones sent off a thousand splendors. Out of another came melodious songs. Out of a third, divine music. Then there were tables set with delicious foods, rare and ripe fruits, inebriating liqueurs, and sweet scents flowing out of fountains. And, finally, dances, games, and a rush of people who ran from one ray to another in search of enjoyment and distractions.

Goldenbeard stood indifferent to that crowd, and Prince Valorous asked where he should go in order to experience a more intense joy.

"Go where pleasure leads you," answered the sage. "Only hurry up, because joy is brief, and the hour is fleeting."

So, the prince entered the fray of pleasure. He wanted to see and taste everything. He filled his bag with precious stones. He took a maiden by the hand and invited her to dance, but after one spin, she vanished, and all he held in his hands was a fistful of air. To console himself, he went into the ray where tables were set, and there he tasted delicious foods and inebriating drinks, such that he went through the other rays staggering and directionless, transported by the throng of people. At one point, he almost got lost. As he felt his limbs overtaken by an invincible torpor, he fell to the ground sleeping.

A cold air shook him, and then, a sudden glare. He opened his eyes and looked around, dazed. The sun was already high over the horizon, and he did not know where he was, nor could he remember what had happened. He felt as if he had just woken up from a long sleep, and that he had been the victim of a beautiful dream.

The shining palace had disappeared, and before his eyes stood a barren mountain made of granite stone. The only thing he remembered was the bridge at his feet, linking the island to the shore— the same bridge he had impatiently crossed the previous evening. His limbs ached, and he was overcome by a sense of fear—fear of being alone. However, he felt reassured when he realized that his faithful Goldenbeard was not far, sitting and meditating on the trunk of a fallen tree.

The prince approached him and asked, "Where is the palace of illusions?"

"It disappeared," said the sage, "as do all the mirages that the gullible crowd runs after."

"But something of it remains," said the prince, remembering that he had filled his bag with precious stones.

As he said this, he turned the bag upside down, but all that fell out were pebbles, muddy soil, and tiny worms. He was so disappointed that he broke down crying.

"Shame on you!" said Goldenbeard. "A prince must not cry. Let's keep going toward life, instead of following the vain fantasies that disperse like smoke in the wind."

And down they went toward their villa. Here, the prince was able to console himself for his lost illusions by embracing his doll and holding her tight, afraid that she might disappear just like the images he had seen in the night.

Goldenbeard shook his head, saying: "That, too, is an illusion, and it will disappear like everything else. Listen to me, Prince Valorous, do not trust false appearances. Prepare yourself instead for new journeys and new adventures."

The prince placed the doll in her velvet case with great care and said, "I am ready."

Their coach was waiting outside the villa, and the prince and Goldenbeard went off through valleys and mountains until they stopped in a busy city teeming with life and work. Instead of palaces shining with gems, there were huge buildings with tall smokestacks releasing a noxious smoke. The throngs of people filling the streets were shabbily dressed. Shirtless men pulled heavy carts and carried enormous loads. Gaunt women in tattered clothes stopped passersby asking for alms.

"I don't like it," said the prince. "Let's leave."

"This is life," said Goldenbeard.

"Life is very ugly," answered the prince. "I prefer illusion. Let's go, then. Let's go now."

But further on, all they saw was even more misery. Groups of tattered children were fighting with each other, and grown men were arguing over nothing, with one stabbing the other with a knife. Later, sick people were heading toward the hospital to be treated.

"Come on, come on," said the prince. "Let's get far away from all this misery. Isn't there a king in this country? Let's go see him. I am tired of witnessing such a spectacle."

The wise Goldenbeard answered: "There is no king here. At one time, this region was divided into little kingdoms always at war with one another. Tired of all those wars, the people organized a revolution, and all the reigning families were chased away and took refuge in a valley that is now called the Valley of Kings. Here, the people are in charge, but not even this change has brought about peace. War goes on, instead, and it will always be so in countries where hatred rules, instead of love.

"Let us go, then, to the Valley of the Kings," said the prince. "Let us go far away from all this misery."

"Perhaps in that valley misery will be hidden, but it will be no less painful," answered Goldenbeard. "Still, if that is what you wish, let us go there."

They left the suffering kingdom, traveling through endlessly long plains, and then through quiet and mysterious forests, until they arrived at a pleasant valley, surrounded by green hills. Here, in the middle of flowery gardens, they could see the whiteness of sumptuous palaces, and princely villas in a wide variety of architectural styles, all of them beautiful and elegant.

"Finally!" exclaimed the prince. "Here is a pleasant place, and it feels like a different world. I am actually able to breathe better. Let us stop here for a while to regain the strength lost during those horrors we saw."

They asked if there was a villa they could use, and when people learned that this was Prince Valorous, they were offered very many options. More than ten landlords fought over the honor of hosting him, and the prince chose an elegant pavilion at the edge of the wood.

"I will be able to go hunting," he said. "I am tired of being idle."

Goldenbeard's face lit up with joy when he saw that his pupil was considering more manly resolutions, instead of thinking about the doll. Indeed, for a few days, the prince seemed full of bravery and industriousness: he left at dawn on his favorite horse, went into the forest, and chased game that he then brought home in triumph.

In the afternoon, they went to see the dethroned kings who inhabited the valley, but those were very sad visits. Although they lived in a delightful place, the princes sorely missed their past life, their lost power, and their triumph over their enemies, and they complained about their destiny, because their idleness bored them. Around them were just a few faithful followers, and there was no one to praise their feats as in times past.

Their continuous complaints did not amuse Prince Valorous in the least. He was already planning on moving on and continuing his journey, when his new friends begged him to participate in the feast of the kings. This feast was celebrated every year on the first day of spring. All the kings gathered together in the central park, exchanged gifts and greetings, and sat at a sumptuous banquet in the shade of ancient trees.

On the appointed day, the park was decorated for the celebration. As brightly colored flags waved in the wind, all the kings, queens, and princes arrived accompanied by their golden crew wearing clothes in every color imaginable, and sporting brocade coats and pendants studded with jewels. On the lawns, musical bands played the national anthems of every country in attendance, and everyone forgot their cares and grudges during that hour of celebration. Smiling, Prince Valorous moved from one group of people to another, pausing to greet and converse with his friends. But all of a sudden, he stopped in his tracks when he saw a young woman in tears sitting on a bench covered with ivy. Her eyes, hair, and lips looked just like those of Acacia Blossom's doll, the doll that now lay forgotten in the velvet case. As if impelled by a higher power, he approached her and said: "Who are you, O beautiful maiden, and why are you crying in the middle of a celebration?"

"I am the daughter of the King of France," she said sobbing. "Forgive me if I sadden you, but my sorrow can find no relief."

"Do you perchance long for your lost kingdom?" asked the prince. "Not in the least."

"For your past riches and splendors, then?"

"What are riches for? They do not bring happiness."

"Have you perhaps lost your fiancé?"

"No, not at all," said the princess. "My sorrow is without hope. I adore my mother, and she is ill and will die."

"I shall save her, I promise you," said the prince, lovingly taking her hand. "Just tell me what I must do."

The princess shook her head with an incredulous gesture and answered: "The sages have said that there is no remedy for my mother's ailment. The only thing that could keep her alive is water from the Fountain of Immortality."

"Tell me where it is, and even if it is at the other end of the world, I will go and get it."

"It is useless," said the princess. "Other knights have gone and never returned. You are young and handsome. Spare your own life."

"And what if I brought you that marvelous water?"

"I would give my life to save my mother."

"Will you be my bride?" asked the prince.

"I promise," answered the princess. "But for pity's sake, do not risk your life for such a dangerous and vain undertaking."

"Not for nothing is my name Prince Valorous. Tell me only where the water that gives immortality is found."

"In the Kingdom of Caves," answered the princess. "Here is a map with the path that you must follow. Beware that the cave where the water flows is guarded by a ferocious bear. Once again, I beg you: give up this dangerous task."

"Never," said the prince. "Tell me your name, and with your name on my lips, I do not fear the snares of all the bears in the world."

"Stella," answered the princess.

When the prince heard that name, he was ecstatic and said: "Don't you know that your name was carved in my heart before I even met you? I have loved your image that I always carry with me and whose name is Stella. A good fairy certainly sent me on your path. Farewell. You will see me again soon, and I will succeed. I promise you this."

The beautiful maiden followed him with a smile full of hope, while the prince, running as if he had wings on his feet, went to Goldenbeard to tell him about his adventure. He had found his Stella—not the one he had brought along with him in a velvet case, but the daughter of the King of France, and she would be his bride if he could bring her the water of immortality.

"I will start on my journey immediately," he added. "But you who are so wise, you must help me in this task."

"The fountain that you are seeking has run out," said the sage. "You might be able to collect the last drops if the bear guarding the door will allow it. Beware not to lose your own precious life."

"Tell me what I must do."

"Proceed with courage, always. Take this bundle and this vial, filled with a marvelous fluid. Perhaps they will be helpful to you."

"What about you? Are you abandoning me?"

"I am forbidden from entering that Kingdom of Caves, but I will follow you at a distance, and my prayers will accompany you."

It had been a long time since Prince Valorous had felt so happy and full of courage as he did on the day he started traveling toward the Kingdom of Caves. By this point, Acacia Blossom's doll was just a dream, and Princess Stella was now his reality, and the only hope in his life. He would have faced one thousand dangers just so he could bring her the miraculous water. Armed to his teeth, he straddled his most handsome and most resilient horse, carrying with him Goldenbeard's gifts. And off he went, galloping toward that sacred kingdom.

Initially, things went well, but the closer he got to the Kingdom of Caves, the more difficult and muddy the roads became. A cold feeling penetrated his bones, his hands were so stiff that he almost let the reins drop, and he feared that he would get stuck on the road like a statue of ice, unable to go any farther. Then he thought of Princess Stella, and his energy was renewed. But soon, the cold stung him with such force that he felt lost and about to freeze to death. Suddenly, he remembered Goldenbeard's bundle, untied it, and to his surprise found the pelt of a polar bear, which he wore to protect himself from the cold. Within five minutes, he was turned into the most perfect polar bear, a worthy dweller of those frozen lands.

Because the horse was slowing him down, he left him in a cave, placing a fir branch at the entrance so that he could find him on this way back. Moving slowly and stumbling on the muddy road, he headed toward the cave marked on his map. The cold was becoming ever more intense, but now that he was changed into a bear, he did not fear it. He proceeded among the rocks, crossing icy streams and snowy fields.

All of a sudden, he found himself in front of a polar bear sitting at the entrance of a cave. Inside that cave was the water he was seeking. He made an attempt to enter, but the bear blocked his path with a grunt that meant: "No entrance."

"Why?" asked the prince. "We are brothers, let me through."

"For what purpose?"

"To drink. I am very thirsty."

"It is impossible."

"You will yield to force!" And the prince moved to attack that beast.

"You cannot kill me: I am immortal. But no one else will be, and this is why I am here, standing guard."

The prince remembered the vial that Goldenbeard had given him, on which a single word was written: NARCOTIC. And he said: "I too possess a marvelous water, and, being more generous than you are, I am offering you a few drops."

"It will not make anyone immortal, the way mine does."

"This is much better," said the prince. "My water makes one happy."

The bear, bored with always guarding the cave, and feeling quite unhappy, said: "Let me taste it, and if what you say is true, I will let you enter the cave."

The prince poured the contents of his vial into the mouth of the bear, who immediately fell asleep, like a dead weight. The spell was broken, and Valorous seized this moment to enter the cave and take the last few drops of the water of immortality. There was barely enough for one person. He collected it in the little vial in great haste and left running.

As soon as he was out of the kingdom of the caves, he reached his horse and went off at a gallop without turning back, swift as the air, and filled with cheerful thoughts. He made it all the way to the Valley of the Kings and stopped before the villa of Princess Stella. The princess was next to her mother, who was wasting away with every passing day. She did not cry, because she was hoping to see Prince Valorous return. When she heard the gallop of his horse, she rushed to the door, her beautiful face beaming with joy.

"What about the marvelous water?" she asked.

"Here it is," answered the triumphant prince, handing her the little vial he held between his fingers.

Stella took it eagerly and gripped it tightly in her hand, like a treasure.

"Thank you, Prince Valorous," she said, "Whatever happens next, I will be your bride."

They went into the house, and her first thought was to hand her mother the miracle-working liqueur.

"First you too must drink half of it," said her mother.

"It is barely enough for one person," murmured the prince.

"I do not want it, then," said the mother. "What would be the use of immortality if someday I should see the death of all my loved ones, and if I should see even you die, beloved daughter? What would I do in this world without true affection? It would be a terrible life. Let destiny be fulfilled, and in any case, the joy of seeing Stella entrusted to Prince Valorous will let me close my eyes in peace."

There was a gentle fight between mother and daughter over the fateful water, but at one point the vial broke and the water spilled

onto the carpet. It was the last drop, and human beings from that day on were no longer able to become immortal.

Informed by Goldenbeard of the healing of Prince Valorous and of his engagement, the King of the Rising Sun sent a retinue of foot soldiers and knights in triumphal chariots to meet the bride and groom. Parties and banquets were prepared. Princess Stella and Prince Valorous, happy and content, started toward the Kingdom of the Rising Sun, and Acacia Blossom's doll was forever left forgotten in her velvet case.

Goldenfeather and Finestlead

I.

Goldenfeather was an orphan who lived with her grandfather in a hut in the woods. The grandfather was a charcoal burner, and she helped him gather branches and make coal. The little girl grew into a good person, beloved by her friends and by the old ladies from nearby farms. And she was beautiful: as beautiful as a queen.

One spring day, she saw a white butterfly on the carnations of her windowsill and held the butterfly between her fingers.

"Let me go, for pity's sake!"

Goldenfeather let the butterfly go.

"Thank you, beautiful girl. What is your name?"

"Goldenfeather."

"My name is Hawthorn White. I am going to lay my caterpillars in a faraway land. Maybe I will reward you one day."

And the butterfly flew away.

Another day, while she was walking in the middle of the forest, Goldenfeather grabbed a beautiful snow-white dandelion puff carried off by the wind, and as she was tearing apart its light silk, she heard, "Let me go, for pity's sake!"

Goldenfeather let the puff go.

"Thank you, beautiful girl. What is your name?"

"Goldenfeather."

"Thank you, Goldenfeather. My name is Achene of the Cardoon. I am going to lay my seeds in a faraway land. Maybe I will reward you one day."

And the dandelion puff flew away.

Another day, Goldenfeather grabbed an emerald scarab within the heart of a rose.

"Let me go, for pity's sake!"

Goldenfeather let the scarab go.

"Thank you, beautiful girl. What is your name?"

"Goldenfeather."

"Thank you, Goldenfeather. My name is Golden Beetle. I am seeking the roses of a faraway land. Maybe I will reward you one day.

And the beetle flew away.

II.

When she was about fourteen, something strange happened to Goldenfeather. She started losing weight.

She was still a beautiful girl, blonde and thriving, but she became a little lighter every day.

At first, she was not worried. It amused her, in fact, to let herself go from the branches of the tallest trees and float down ever so slowly, like a sheet of paper. And she used to sing:

> *The only one I adore—is Goldenfeather.*
> *O Goldenfeather,*
> *You beautiful child—you will be queen.*

But with the passing of time, she became so light that her grandfather had to attach four large stones to her skirt so that the wind

would not carry her away. Eventually, the stones were no longer enough, and her grandfather had to shut her in the house.

"Goldenfeather, my poor child, this is a spell."

The old man sighed. And Goldenfeather grew bored, shut inside the house like that.

"Make me fly, grandfather!"

Her grandfather blew air on her, and Goldenfeather rose up lightly all the way up to the ceiling beams.

> O Goldenfeather,
> You beautiful child—you will be queen.

"Goldenfeather, what are you singing?"

"It's not me singing. It's a voice singing within me."

Goldenfeather was, indeed, hearing the words repeated by a sweet voice from far away.

And the old man blew air on her and sighed, "Goldenfeather, my poor child, this is a spell."

III.

One morning, Goldenfeather woke up lighter and more bored than usual.

"Make me fly, grandfather!"

But the old man did not respond.

"Make me fly, grandfather!"

Goldenfeather approached her grandfather's bed. Her grandfather had died.

Goldenfeather wept.

She wept for three days and three nights. At dawn on the fourth day, she wanted to call someone. But as soon as she pulled the front door open a little bit, the wind grabbed her and sent her up higher and higher, like a soap bubble.

Goldenfeather screamed and closed her eyes.

She finally dared open them slowly and looked down through her flowing hair. She was flying dizzyingly high.

She saw the green countryside moving under her, and then silvery rivers, dark forests, cities, towers, and abbeys. They looked like tiny toys.

Goldenfeather again closed her eyes in fear, wrapped herself up in her flowing hair, and rested there, as within the covers of her bed. She let herself be transported.

"Goldenfeather, be brave!"

She opened her eyes. Before her were the butterfly, the beetle, and the dandelion puff.

"The wind brings us with you, Goldenfeather. We will follow you and help you find your destiny."

Goldenfeather felt reborn.

"Thank you, my friends."

> *The only one I adore—is Goldenfeather.*
> *O Goldenfeather,*
> *You beautiful child—you will be queen.*

"Who has been singing in my ear for so long?"

"You will find out this evening, Goldenfeather, when we arrive at the Fairy of Adolescence."

Goldenfeather, the butterfly, the beetle, and the dandelion puff continued on their journey, transported by the wind.

IV.

When evening fell, they arrived at the Fairy of Adolescence. They entered through the open window.

The good Fairy greeted them kindly. She took Goldenfeather by the hand, and together they crossed huge rooms and endless hallways. Then the Fairy took a round mirror out of a golden coffer.

"Look in here."

Goldenfeather looked. She saw a marvelous garden, with palm trees and tropical plants and flowers she had never seen before. And within the garden, she saw a young man dressed like a king and handsome as the sun. The young man sat in a golden carriage that five hundred pairs of oxen could barely pull, and he sang:

> O Goldenfeather,
> You beautiful child—you will be queen.

"The one you see is Finestlead, Prince of the Fortunate Islands, and he is the one who has been calling you for so long with his song. He is the victim of a spell opposite to yours. Five hundred pairs of oxen can barely pull him. He is becoming heavier and heavier. The spell will be broken the moment you two first kiss each other."

The vision disappeared, and the good Fairy gave Goldenfeather three grains of wheat.

"Before reaching the Fortunate Islands, the wind will carry you over three castles. In each castle, an evil fairy will appear to you, trying to lure you with threats or flattery. Each time, you will drop one of these grains."

Goldenfeather thanked the Fairy, leapt out of the window with her companions, and started back on her journey, transported by the wind.

V.

Toward evening, they arrived near the first castle. On its towers, the Colorful Fairy appeared, gesturing with her hands. Goldenfeather felt herself drawn by a mysterious force and began to descend slowly.

She seemed to recognize the smiling faces of people she knew in the gardens—her playmates, the old ladies of her native forest, and her grandfather were all greeting her.

But the beetle reminded her of the Fairy of Adolescence's warning, and Goldenfeather dropped a grain of wheat. The smiling people suddenly turned into demons and witches crowned with hissing snakes.

As Goldenfeather was lifted up high again with her companions, she realized that what she saw was the Castle of Lies and that the grain she dropped was the grain of Prudence.

They traveled for two more days and arrived at the second castle toward evening.

It was a bile-colored building, striped with the tint of blood. The Green Fairy was furiously swaying on its towers and a crowd of livid people gestured menacingly from the crenellations and the courtyards.

Goldenfeather began to descend, attracted by a mysterious force. Terrified, she dropped the second grain. As soon as the grain touched the ground, the castle became golden, and the Fairy and her guests turned benevolent and smiling, greeting Goldenfeather with their outstretched hands. Goldenfeather was lifted up again and resumed her journey, transported by the wind. She understood that what she had dropped was the grain of Goodness.

She traveled on and on and arrived at the third castle two days later. It was a marvelous building, made of gold and precious jewels.

The Blue Fairy appeared on the towers, gesturing benevolently toward Goldenfeather.

Goldenfeather felt herself drawn by a mysterious force. As she approached the ground, she heard a confusing noise of laughter,

songs, and music. She could also see big groups of magnificent ladies and gentlemen in the gardens, busy with eating, drinking, dancing, jousting, and theater.

Goldenfeather was dazzled and was just about to descend, but
the beetle reminded her of the Fairy of Adolescence's warning,
and she begrudgingly dropped the third grain of wheat. As soon as
the grain touched the ground, the castle turned into a hovel, the
Blue Fairy into a fearsome hag, and the ladies and gentlemen into

desperate paupers dressed in rags, weeping and running amid the stones and thorn bushes. Goldenfeather soared into the air again and understood that what she saw was the Castle of Desires, and that the dropped grain was the grain of Wisdom.

She continued on her way, transported by the wind.

The butterfly, the beetle, and the dandelion puff followed her faithfully and gathered all the friends that they came across along the way. Thus, Goldenfeather soon had a retinue of colorful butterflies, clouds of white puffs, and dazzling armies of emerald beetles.

They traveled on and on, until the land came to an end, and Goldenfeather saw an infinite blue expanse below her. It was the sea.

The wind was calming down, and Goldenfeather sometimes descended all the way to the water, until she touched the white seafoam with her hair. When she cried out in fear, the ten thousand butterflies and the ten thousand beetles lifted her back up with the flutter of their tiny wings.

They traveled this way for seven days.

At the dawn of the eighth day, they could see on the horizon the golden minarets and the tall palm trees of the Fortunate Islands.

VI.

At the royal palace, everyone was desperate. The floor of the Grand Council Hall had collapsed under Prince Finestlead's weight, and he was immersed up to his belt in the mosaic decorating the floor. Blond, with blue eyes and all dressed in red velvet, Finestlead was as handsome as a god, but the spell was becoming more perverse with each passing day.

By now the young man's weight was such that all of the oxen in the kingdom were unable to move him a single inch. Doctors, wizards, fortune-tellers, necromancers, alchemists, had all been called around the spellbound heir—but in vain.

> *The only one I adore—is Goldenfeather.*
> *O Goldenfeather,*
> *You beautiful child—you will be queen.*

And Finestlead was sinking deeper and deeper, like a bronze mortar into the sand of the sea. A wizard had foreseen that every effort to help him would be utterly useless, unless help came from the crossing of certain benevolent stars. The queen kept running to the window, consulting the astrologers on the towers with great insistence.

"Master Simon! What do you see on the horizon? What do you see?"

"Nothing, Your Majesty. . . . The Christian Fleet returning from the Holy Land."

And Finestlead was still sinking.

"Master Simon, what do you see?"

"Nothing, Your Majesty. . . . A flock of migrating herons."

And Finestlead was sinking deeper and deeper.

"Master Simon, what do you see?"

"Nothing, Your Majesty. . . . A Venetian galley loaded with ivory."

The king, the queen, the ministers, the ladies . . . all were on the brink of despair.

At this point, only Finestlead's head could be seen emerging from the floor, and as he sank deeper and deeper, he kept on singing:

> O Goldenfeather,
> You beautiful child—you will be queen.

All of a sudden, Master Simon's voice could be heard announcing: "Your Majesty! . . . I see a comet on the horizon! A star that shines in the middle of the afternoon!"

Everyone ran to the window, but before they could even get there, the great glass windows in the back of the hall opened by magic, and Goldenfeather appeared with her retinue before the astonished Court.

The dandelion puffs had woven a dress made of tulle for her, and the butterflies had colored it with gemstones. The ten thousand beetles had turned into ten thousand emerald-clad pageboys and flanked the young woman, who entered smiling, as beautiful and majestic as a goddess.

As soon as Finestlead received Goldenfeather's first kiss, he came to as if from a dream, and jumped to his feet, finally free and disenchanted, while many cries of joy could be heard from the exultant Court.

The feasting that followed had never been seen before, and eight days later, Goldenfeather, the charcoal maker, married the Prince of the Fortunate Islands.

The Three Talismans

When every chicken had its teeth
And all the snow that fell was black
(Children, children, listen up)
There was then, there was . . . there was . . .

. . . an old peasant who had three sons. When he felt the hour of his death draw near, he called them to his bedside for one last goodbye.

"Dear children, I am not rich, but I have a precious talisman for each of my sons. To you, Cassandrino, who are a poet and the poorest of the three, I leave this threadbare bag: each time you stick your hand in it, you will find one hundred coins. To you, Sansonetto, who are a farmer and will have many mouths to feed, I leave this wrinkled tablecloth: all you have to do is lay it on the ground or on a table, and it will be covered with dishes for as many people as you want. To you, Oddo, who are a merchant and must travel very often, I leave this cloak. All you have to do is put it on your shoulders and hold it by its corners with your arms extended, and it will make you invisible and take you wherever you want."

The good father died shortly afterward, and the three sons, crying, took their talismans and went their separate ways.

Cassandrino arrived in the city, bought a marvelous palace, clothing, jewels, and horses, and began to live the life of a great lord. Everyone thought him an exiled prince, and he himself started to believe it—so much so that he wished to meet the king. He wore his most luxurious clothes and jewels and went to the royal palace.

A guard stopped him.

"Prince, what do you wish for?"

"To meet the king."

"Give me your name and if His Majesty sees fit, he will receive you."

"No complications, please! Here are one hundred coins."

The guard bowed down to the ground, and Cassandrino left him behind. But at the royal door, four other armed guards stopped him.

"Prince, where are you going?"

"To the king."

"You can't just go visit His Majesty whenever you wish. Say your name, and if the king wants to receive you, you will be let through."

Cassandrino offered one hundred coins to each guard. Still, they hesitated.

"Is it not enough? Take more."

Won over by the gold, the guards let him through, and Cassandrino became friends with the king.

A few days later, the entire Court, entranced, was talking of Cassandrino's fabulous generosity. Everywhere he went, the young man distributed one-hundred-coin tips, so that servants, cooks, housekeepers, butlers, and valets bowed to him and rejoiced. The princess, the king's only daughter, had a personal maid who was paid more than anyone else, but who was also cleverer than the others. This personal maid began to suspect that magic was involved in the prince's generosity. She spoke about it to her mistress while removing her stockings one evening.

"Princess, the foreigner's bag is enchanted. Can't you see how small it is? And yet he pulls thousands of coins out of it every night. We should take it from him."

"We should," agreed the princess. "But how?"

"He sits every night at your left. So, just pour a sleeping potion into his cup. He will fall asleep, and the task will be easy."

And so, it was done. The following evening, during the dessert course, Prince Cassandrino began to nod off, then dropped his head on the tablecloth and fell asleep, to the great surprise of the king and his guests. He was brought to a room in the palace and laid on a bed.

The vigilant maid took Cassandrino's bag and brought it to her mistress. The two then handed the sleeping youth over to four guards, who brought him outside the palace doors and left him in a deserted field. At dawn, Cassandrino woke up freezing and understood that he had been deceived.

"I will seek revenge," he said. So, he left the city and went back to his hometown.

He arrived at the home of his farmer brother, who welcomed him with open arms and had him sit next to the fire with his wife and children.

"Dear brother Cassandrino, where is your enchanted bag?"

"Alas! It was stolen from me, and in the most childish of ways." And he told his brother about his misfortune. "You could help me get it back, though."

"How?"

"By lending me your tablecloth for a little while."

The brother hesitated.

"I beg you! I will only keep it for a few days, and then I will bring it back to you."

Sansonetto gave Cassandrino the enchanted tablecloth, pleading with him to return it safely. Cassandrino went back to the city, wore humble clothing, and showed up at the palace disguised as a cook seeking employment. The Minister of Food looked at him with contempt and disbelief and assigned him the lowest place in the kitchen.

On the day that the king had ordered a gala dinner for the Sultan's ambassadors, Cassandrino told the head chef: "Leave the cooking to me. I promise you a meal the likes of which you have never seen before."

The head chef cackled contemptuously, "Poor crazy servant!"

But Cassandrino insisted with such passion that the head chef said, "Do you swear on your own head?"

"On my own head."

The cooks and the chef went for a walk, and Cassandrino stayed in the kitchen. A few minutes before noon, he went up to the dining hall and lay down the miraculous tablecloth on a corner of the long table.

"Tablecloth! Tablecloth! Prepare a banquet for five hundred people, such as to astonish the king, the Court, and the ambassadors. A banquet such as to confound all the cooks of the earth!"

And here were the finest tablecloths flashing white, sparkling crystals and silverware, and an abundance of the most refined dishes, including fantastic casseroles, exquisite venison, unusual fish, fruits from across the sea, and wines from sun-drenched islands. Lunchtime arrived, and all of the guests were enthusiastic. The king called the head chef and chose to honor him with his compliments before the entire Court. From that day on, the head chef entrusted Cassandrino with the direction of the kitchen, keeping all the praises for himself.

Every day, Cassandrino went up alone to the dining room a few moments before the beginning of each meal. He locked himself in and then left almost immediately—and the royal tables were laden with food.

The servants began to suspect him of witchcraft.

The princess's personal maid, who was more clever than the others, spied on him from a keyhole and saw the sudden appearance of the dishes.

She reported this to her mistress right away.

"Princess! The man with the bag is still in the palace, disguised as a chef, and he owns an enchanted tablecloth that makes entire dinners appear!"

"We must have that tablecloth," said the princess.

"We shall have it!" the maid assured her. And the next night, she broke into the case where Cassandrino kept the wonder-working tablecloth and exchanged it with a regular tablecloth.

The following day, at lunchtime, Cassandrino laid down the tablecloth to no effect and repeated his command in vain. The tables remained empty.

"Here I am, cheated once again! But it doesn't matter. I shall get my revenge!"

So, he left the palace and returned to his hometown, where he went to his merchant brother, who embraced him and asked him about his adventures. Cassandrino confided in him about his unhappy circumstances.

"They stole my bag and the tablecloth, but if you want, you can help me get everything back."

"And how, dear brother?"

"By loaning me the enchanted cloak for a few days."

The merchant hesitated, because the cloak, which made its wearer invisible and abolished every distance, was necessary to him for his business. But Cassandrino implored him so much that he obtained the cloak. With the cloak open and held at its corners by his outstretched arms, it took him but an instant to reach the city, climb up the palace stairs, and enter the princess's room. She was sleeping, and Cassandrino covered her face with the edge of the cloak.

"By the powers of this cloak, I want both of us to be transported to the Fortunate Islands."

The cloak wrapped them both in a dark and swirling cloud, and within a few seconds set them down under a palm grove in those distant islands.

Realizing that she was at the mercy of her enemy, the princess pretended to accept her fate, but she did this just to discover the secret of his power. And she was so good at deception that she soon learned about the powers of the cloak. One night, while Cassandrino was sleeping with the precious cloth folded under his head, she carefully slipped it out from under him.

"By the power of this cloak, I wish to be transported to the palace of my father, the king."

Cassandrino woke up just as the cloak was wrapping the princess in a dark and swirling cloud and carrying her off into the blue sky toward her father's kingdom.

"Here I am once more robbed by that sly woman," he said, and started sobbing in despair.

He spent many months on the island, living on fruit alone. One day, while wandering along the seashore, he discovered a tree bearing enormous red fruit. He ate one and found it delicious, but he soon felt an annoying itch throughout his body. He glanced at his hands and at his arms, and when he looked at himself reflected in a pool of water, he saw his body entirely covered in green scales.

"Goodness! Woe is me! What is this?"

And touching his skin, he found it to be as scaly as a snake's. Cassandrino was tempted to eat some of the yellow fruit growing on a nearby tree, and right then, with another itch, his green scales disappeared little by little, and his skin became white again. So, he started alternating the two types of fruit, and amused himself by turning green and then white again by turns.

After several months in exile, Cassandrino spotted a pirate ship crossing the horizon. Cassandrino yelled and screamed so much that the pirates approached the beach and welcomed him aboard. Before leaving the island, however, the young man picked three fruits from each tree and put them in his pockets.

He then came home and returned to the princess's city. The following Sunday, he disguised himself as a pilgrim, placed a little stool on the steps of the church where the king's daughter went to Mass, and placed the three beautiful fruits that made those who eat them turn green on top of the stool.

The princess walked by, followed by her servant, and stopped in admiration, but she did not recognize the false pilgrim. She turned to her servant and said, "Tersilla, go buy those apples."

The woman approached the pilgrim.

"How much do you want for those fruits?"

"Three hundred coins."

"What did you say?"

"Three hundred coins."

"Are you mad? One hundred coins per fruit?"

"If you want them, buy them. Otherwise, words are cheap."

The woman went back to her mistress.

"Three hundred coins! You were right not to buy them."

And they entered the church for Mass.

But during the ceremony, the princess could not stop thinking of the pilgrim's fruits as she knelt before the altar with her hands joined in prayer. As soon as she went outside, she stopped again to admire them, then told her servant: "Go buy those fruits for three hundred coins. I will make up for the expense with the miraculous bag."

The woman approached the pilgrim and spoke to him.

"Please forgive me, my dear. I am now asking for six hundred coins for those fruits, and not three hundred."

"Are you kidding me?"

"You should have bought them earlier. Now the price has doubled."

The woman went first to her mistress, then back to the pilgrim, and made the purchase. At dinner, the fruits were presented on a golden tray and brought on everyone's admiration. When it was time for the dessert course, the king took one fruit for himself and then gave one to the queen and another to the princess, and they all found them delicious. But the three had not even finished a single fruit when they started looking at one another, disturbed to find themselves turning green and completely covered in snake-like scales. They were terrified and on the brink of despair.

The king, the queen, and the princess were carried to their rooms, and the terrible news spread across the kingdom. The most famous doctors were consulted, but in vain. A proclamation was therefore made: anyone who could make the royal family's green skin disappear would obtain the princess's hand or, if already married, half the kingdom.

Cassandrino let the doctors, the surgeons, the enchantresses, and the fortune-tellers come and go, and after a few days presented himself at the royal palace.

He was admitted into the sickroom.

"Do you promise to heal us?"

"I promise."

"And when will the cure begin?"

"Even immediately, if you'd like."

Cassandrino had the king strip down to his belt. Then, with gloved hands, he took a bunch of nettles out of a basket and began to whip the king's shoulders.

"Enough! Enough!" screamed the king.

"Not yet, Your Majesty."

He then moved on to the queen and repeated the shoulder whipping.

When the two sovereigns were put back to bed, half-dead, Cassandrino gave them the other fruit from the faraway islands. Their faces began to whiten, slowly, and the scales became thinner and eventually disappeared altogether.

The king and queen were exultant.

It was now the princess's turn.

Cassandrino wanted to be alone with her and locked himself in her room.

Soon the heartrending screams and moans began.

"Help! Enough! Enough!"

The cure went on.

"I am dying! Enough! Help! For pity's sake!"

After an hour, Cassandrino left the room, leaving the princess half-dead.

"And her skin?" asked the king and queen.

"I will whiten it tomorrow. Tomorrow, I shall return to complete the cure."

Cassandrino went to visit an abbot friend of his and said to him: "Tomorrow, around noon, come to the royal palace to give confession to the princess, for she is in danger of death."

The abbot promised he would be there.

The next day, Cassandrino went to the palace.

"Holy Crown, today I will give the princess her last treatment, but since she might die from it. . . ."

"Dear God! What are you saying?" screamed the king and queen.

"I thought it a good idea to call an abbot for the last rites. He will be here around noon."

Cassandrino then went up to the princess.

"Today, I will give you your last treatment, but since it might be fatal to you, an abbot has been called so that you can die in peace with your conscience."

The princess's eyes were glazed over with fear. The abbot arrived, and he was left alone with the princess while Cassandrino waited in a small room next door.

When the priest left the princess's bedroom, Cassandrino said: "My friend, please lend me your clothes for a few moments."

"That would be an offense to the habit."

"Fear not. I will do nothing sacrilegious. It is for an excellent cause."

Cassandrino put on the priestly habit and went to the princess, who was moaning in her bed.

"Dear child, I am afraid you forgot a few things when you confessed your sins. . . . Think about it, search your soul a bit deeper. . . . Remember that you might be about to meet the Supreme Judge."

The princess went pale and sobbed.

"Let's see," said Cassandrino, imitating his friend's voice. "Don't you remember taking . . . Or rather . . . Stealing something?"

"Dear Father!" sobbed the princess. "I stole a wonder-working bag from a foreign prince."

"You must return it! Entrust it to me, and I will make sure it gets to him."

The princess pointed with a tired gesture to a silver case, and Cassandrino took the bag.

"Is there anything else, anything else at all that you remember?"

"Ah! Father, I have stolen an enchanted tablecloth from that same foreigner. Take it. You'll find it in that ivory box."

"Is there anything else, anything else at all?"

"A cloak, Father! A magical cloak, from the same foreigner. It is there, in that cedar closet. . . ."

And Cassandrino took the cloak.

"Good," said the false priest. "Now bite on this fruit: it will do you good."

The princess bit into the fruit and immediately her green scales began to thin out, and eventually disappeared altogether. Then, Cassandrino took off his wig and his habit.

"Princess, do you recognize me?"

"Have mercy, have mercy! Forgive me for everything! I have been punished enough!"

The king and queen entered their daughter's room, and the king, seeing her healed, embraced the doctor.

"I offer you the princess's hand. It is yours by right."

"Thank you, Your Majesty! I am already engaged to a girl from my hometown."

"Then you have the right to half my kingdom."

"Thank you, Your Majesty! I would not know what to do with it! I am content with this old bag, this tablecloth, and this threadbare cloak. . . ."

Cassandrino, making himself invisible, flew home, returned the talismans to his brothers, and, after marrying a woman from his hometown, he lived happily in the countryside, never again endeavoring to have any more adventures.

The Dance of the Gnomes

When the dawn was used to rising,
Used to rising in the evening,
And the sparrows could all speak,
There was then, there was . . . there was . . .

. . . a widow married to a widower. The widower had a daughter from his first wife, and the widow had a daughter from her first husband. The widower's daughter's name was Serena, and the widow's daughter's name was Gordiana. The stepmother hated Serena, who was beautiful and kind, and gave everything to Gordiana, who was ugly and mean.

The family lived in a princely castle, three miles away from the village, and their road went through a crossroads in the forest among the ancient beech trees. Whenever there was a full moon, tiny gnomes danced around the crossroads and played terrible pranks on the night travelers.

On a Sunday evening after dinner, the stepmother, who knew all about the gnomes, told her daughter: "Serena, I forgot my prayer book in the village church. Go get it for me."

"Mother, please forgive me . . . it is night."

"The moon is brighter than the sun."

"Mother, I am afraid! I will go tomorrow morning at dawn."

"I am telling you to go!" replied the stepmother.

"Mother, let Gordiana come with me."

"Gordiana is staying here to keep me company. Off you go!"

Serena grew quiet, resigned herself to her stepmother's decision, and went on her way. She arrived at the woods and slowed her pace, pressing her scapular to her chest with her two hands.

There, among the trees, was the wide crossroads, illuminated by the full moon.

And there were gnomes dancing in the middle of the road.

Holding her breath, Serena observed them from among the trees. They were hunchbacked and crippled like little old men, small like children, and they sported long reddish beards, funny red-and-green jackets, and whimsical-looking hats. They danced in circles, and their shrill chant was accompanied by the cries of night birds. Serena grew pale at the thought of walking among them, but there was no other way: she could not go home without her stepmother's prayer book. She steeled herself against the fear that shook inside her and went on at a steady pace.

As soon as they saw her, the green gnomes separated from the red ones and moved to the sides of the road, as if to let her through. When the child was among them, they enclosed her in a circle and began dancing. One gnome gave her a mushroom and a fern.

"Beautiful child, dance with us!"

"Gladly, if it should please you."

So, Serena danced by the light of the moon, with such sweet grace that the gnomes stopped in their circle, admiring her enthusiastically.

"Oh! what a beautiful, graceful child!" said a gnome.

A second one said, "May she become twice as beautiful and graceful!"

A third one said, "Oh! What a sweet and kind child!"

A fourth one said, "May she become twice as sweet and kind!"

A fifth said, "And may a pearl fall from her left ear with every word that comes out of her mouth."

A sixth one said, "And may she turn anything she wants into gold."

"Let it be so! Let it be so! Let it be so!" all of them yelled with a happy and ringing voice.

The gnomes went back to their dizzying dance, holding hands, then broke the circle, and disappeared. Serena continued on her way, arrived at the village, and had to wake up the sexton because the church was closed.

But, lo and behold, at every word she said a pearl fell from her left ear, bounced on her shoulder, and dropped to the ground. The sexton started gathering them all in the palm of his hand. Serena got the book and returned to her father's castle. The stepmother looked at her in astonishment: Serena was shining with a beauty never seen before.

"Did nothing bad happen to you on the way?"

"Nothing, mother."

And she told her everything in detail. And with every word, a pearl fell from her left ear.

The stepmother was green with envy.

"And my prayer book?"

"Here it is, mother."

The worn-out leather and copper binding had turned into gold adorned with diamonds.

The stepmother was dumbfounded.

She then decided to try the same fate for her daughter, Gordiana. The following Sunday, at the same time, she told her daughter to go get her book in the village church.

"All alone? At night? Mother, are you mad?"

And Gordiana shrugged.

"You must obey, darling, and it will be a wonderful thing for you, I promise."

"Why don't you go yourself instead!"

Gordiana was not used to obeying and threw a tantrum, so her mother was obliged to beat her to get her out of the house and on her way.

When Gordiana arrived at the crossroads, which was silvery with moonlight, the little dancing gnomes moved into two lines on the sides of the road, and then enclosed her in a circle. One of the gnomes came forward, offered the girl a mushroom and a fern, and politely invited her to dance.

"I dance with princes and barons. I do not dance with ugly toads such as yourselves."

And she tossed the fern and the mushroom and tried to open the chain of little dancers by punching and kicking.

"What an ugly and deformed child!" said a gnome.

A second one said, "May she become twice as mean and rude."

"And may she be a hunchback!"

"And may she be a cripple!"

"And may a scorpion crawl out of her left ear with every word she speaks."

"And may everything she touches be covered with drool."

"Let it be so! Let it be so! Let it be so!" they all yelled in a loud and angry voice.

The gnomes went back to dancing, holding each other's hand, then broke the chain and disappeared.

Gordiana shrugged, arrived at the church, took the book, and returned to the castle.

When her mother saw her, she screamed.

"Gordiana, dear daughter, who ruined you this way?"

"You did, wretched mother, when you exposed me to bad luck."

And with every word she uttered, a forked-tailed scorpion crawled down her body. She drew the book out of her pocket and gave it to her mother, but the woman dropped it with a scream of horror.

"How disgusting! It is all filthy with drool!"

The mother was desperate about her daughter, who was now crippled and hunchbacked, uglier and meaner than before. So, she led her into her bedroom and entrusted her to the care of doctors, who worked in vain to heal her.

Meanwhile, the fame of Serena's goodness and dazzling beauty had spread throughout the world, and she received marriage proposals from princes and barons everywhere. However, her evil stepmother rejected every marriage prospect.

The King of Persegonia did not trust his ambassadors, and wanted to go personally to the famed beauty's castle. He was so taken by Serena's sweet charm that he immediately asked for her hand in marriage.

The stepmother was choking with bile, but she behaved respectfully toward the king and appeared happy about that stroke of luck. Already, however, she was hatching the plan of replacing Serena with her own daughter, Gordiana.

The wedding was to take place the following week. The next day, the king sent his fiancée earrings, bracelets, and priceless jewels.

The royal procession arrived to collect the princess. The stepmother covered her daughter Gordiana with jewels and locked Serena inside a cedar trunk.

The king descended from his golden coach and opened the door to let his fiancée in. Gordiana's face was covered with a thick veil, and she was silent at the bridegroom's sweet words.

"Dear mother-in-law, why does the bride not answer me?"

"She is shy, Your Majesty."

"And yet the other day she was so nice to me."

"The solemnity of this day is leaving her speechless."

The king looked at his bride with affection.

"Serena, uncover your face, so that I may see you for just a moment!"

"It is impossible, Your Majesty!" the stepmother interrupted. "The cold air of the coach would ruin her. After the wedding she will reveal herself."

The king was beginning to worry.

They continued toward the church, and already the mother was delighted to see her evil plot come to fruition.

But as they passed by a stream, Gordiana, careless and impatient, leaned forward saying, "Mother, I am thirsty!"

She had barely said three words when three black scorpions came crawling down her white silk gown.

The king and the father-in-law jumped to their feet, horrified, and tore the veil off the bride. Gordiana's horrible, ferocious face appeared.

"Your Majesty, these two evil women wanted to deceive us."

The father-in-law and the king stopped the procession in the middle of the road. The king mounted his horse and went back to his fiancée's castle, alone and at a brisk gallop.

He climbed up the stairs and wandered the halls, calling in a loud voice. "Serena! Serena! Where are you?"

"I am here, Your Majesty!"

"Where?"

"In the cedar trunk!"

The king pried the trunk open with the tip of his sword and lifted the lid. Serena jumped to her feet, pale and beautiful. The king lifted her in his arms, placed her on his horse, and went back to where the procession was awaiting him. Serena took her place in the royal coach, between her father and her fiancé.

The royal wedding was celebrated.

About the stepmother and her evil daughter, who had both run away into the woods, no one ever heard anything again.

■ Bibliography

Earliest Available Editions of the Fairy Tales Translated in This Volume

Capuana, Luigi. "Piuma-d'-Oro." *Il Raccontafiabe (Seguito al C'era una volta)*. Florence: Bemporad, 1894. Pp. 11–32.

———. "Spera di sole" *"C'era una volta . . . Fiabe."* Milan: Treves, 1882. Pp. 1–22.

Collodi (Carlo Lorenzini). "Pelle d'asino." *I racconti delle fate voltati in italiano da C. Collodi*. Florence: Paggi, 1876. Pp. 75–92.

Comparetti, Domenico. "Il figliuolo del re, maiale." *Novelline popolari italiane*. Vol. I. Turin: Loescher, 1875. Pp. 38–39.

———. "I melagrani." *Novelline popolari italiane*. Vol. I. Turin: Loescher, 1875. Pp. 43–45.

———. "Zuccaccia." *Novelline popolari italiane*. Vol. I. Turin: Loescher, 1875. Pp. 244–253.

Cordelia (Virginia Tedeschi Treves). "La bambola del principe Valoroso." *L'ultima fata. Fiabe di Cordelia*. Florence: Bemporad, 1909. Pp. 199–242.

———. "Occhi di fuoco." *L'ultima fata. Fiabe di Cordelia*. Florence: Bemporad, 1909. Pp. 83–102.

D'Annunzio, Gabriele. "La canzone della ricotta insanguinata." *Cronaca bizantina*, January 31, 1886. Pp. 4–5.

———. "La figlia della Borea." *Parabole e novelle*. Naples: Bideri, 1914. Pp. 211–224.

———. "Le palombe." *Cronaca bizantina*, January 10, 1886. P. 6.

Deledda, Grazia. "I tre talismani." *Il Paradiso dei Bambini* (December 1893): 395–396.

———. "Nostra Signora del Buon Consiglio. Fiaba Sarda." *Il Paradiso dei Bambini* 43–45 (November 1892): 347–350 (43); 357–358 (44); 358 (45).

Gozzano, Guido. "I tre talismani." *Il Corriere dei Piccoli* II, no. 29 (July 17, 1910): 5–7.

———. "La danza degli gnomi." *Il Corriere dei Piccoli* II, no. 18 (May 1, 1910): 5–6.

———. "Piumadoro e Piombofino." *Il Corriere dei Piccoli* I, no. 31 (July 25, 1909): 5–6.

Perodi, Emma. "Il velo della Madonna." *Le novelle della nonna: Fiabe fantastiche*. Rome: Perino, 1893. Pp. 707–712.

———. "La matrigna di Lavella." *Le novelle della nonna: Fiabe fantastiche*. Rome: Perino, 1893. Pp. 211–224.

———. "La mula della badessa Sofia." *Le novelle della nonna: Fiabe fantastiche*. Rome: Perino, 1893. Pp. 243–256.

Yorick (Pietro Coccoluto Ferrigni). "Le fate." *Il libro delle fate. Nuova traduzione di Yorick (P. C. Ferrigni)*. Milan: Tipografia del Corriere della Sera, 1891. Pp. 57–60.

Other Sources

Basile, Giambattista. *The Tale of Tales, or Entertainment for Little Ones*. Trans. Nancy Canepa. Detroit: Wayne State University Press, 2007.

Boero, Pino, and Carmine De Luca. *La letteratura per l'infanzia*. Bari: Laterza, 1995.

Bottigheimer, Ruth. *Fairy Tales: A New History*. Albany: State University of New York Press, 2009.

Calvino, Italo. *Italian Folktales*. Trans. George Martin. San Diego: Harcourt, 1980.

Canepa, Nancy. "The Formation of the Literary Fairy Tale in Early Modern Italy, 1550–1636." *Fairy Tale World*. Ed. Andrew Teverson. New York, Routledge, 2019. Pp. 58–67.

———. *From Court to Forest: Giambattista Basile's* Lo cunto de li cunti *and the Birth of the Literary Fairy Tale*. Detroit: Wayne State University Press, 1999.

Capuana, Luigi. "Three Fables from Capuana's *C'era una volta*." Trans. Santi Buscemi. *Italica* 86, no. 3 (2009): 500–533.

Capuana, Luigi, and Jack Zipes. "Luigi Capuana's Search for the New Fairy Tale." *Marvels & Tales* 23, no. 2 (2009): 367–390.

Colin, Mariella. "Children's Literature in France and Italy in the Nineteenth Century: Influences and Exchanges." *Aspects and Issues in the History of Children's Literature*. Ed. Maria Nikolajeva. Westport, CT: Greenwood Press, 1995. Pp. 77–88.

Collingwood, R. G. *The Philosophy of Enchantment: Studies in Folktale, Cultural Criticism, and Anthropology*. Oxford: Clarendon Press, 2005.

Gonzenbach, Laura. *Beautiful Angiola: The Great Treasury of Sicilian Folk and Fairy Tales Collected by Laura Gonzenbach*. Trans. and ed. Jack Zipes. New York: Routledge, 2004.

Gozzi, Carlo. *Fiabe teatrali*. Ed. Alberto Beniscelli. Milan: Garzanti, 2014.

Imbriani, Vittorio, ed. *La novellaja fiorentina: Fiabe e novelline stenografate in Firenze dal dettato popolare*. Bologna: Forni, 1877.

———. *La novellaja milanese: Esempii e panzane lombarde*. Bologna: Fava e Garagnani, 1872.

Johnson, Colin. "An Italian 'Grimm': Domenico Comparetti and the Nationalization of Italian Folktales." *Italica* 87, no. 3 (2010): 462–487.

Maggi, Armando. *Preserving the Spell: Basile's* The Tale of Tales *and Its Afterlife in the Fairy-Tale Tradition*. Chicago: University of Chicago Press, 2015.

Magnanini, Suzanne. *Fairy-Tale Science: Monstrous Generation in the Tales of Straparola and Basile*. Toronto: University of Toronto Press, 2008.

Mazzoni, Cristina. "A Fairy Tale Madonna: Grazia Deledda's 'Our Lady of Good Counsel.'" *Spiritus: A Journal of Christian Spirituality* 19, no. 1 (2019): 131–145.

———. "Of Golden Feathers and Light Reading: Guido Gozzano's 'Piumadoro e Piombofino.'" *Quaderni d'Italianistica* 29, no. 1 (2008): 105–124.

Miele, Gina. "Luigi Capuana: Unlikely Spinner of Fairy Tales?" *Marvels & Tales* 23, no. 2 (2009): 300–324.

Murphy, G. Ronald. *The Owl, the Raven, and the Dove: The Religious Meaning of the Grimms' Fairy Tales.* Oxford: Oxford University Press, 2000.

Perrault, Charles. *The Complete Fairy Tales.* Ed. and trans. Christopher Betts. Oxford: Oxford University Press, 2009.

Pitrè, Giuseppe. *The Collected Sicilian Folk and Fairy Tales of Giuseppe Pitrè.* Ed. and trans. Jack Zipes and Joseph Russo. New York: Routledge, 2009.

Stewart-Steinberg, Suzanne. *The Pinocchio Effect: On Making Italians, 1860–1920.* Chicago: University of Chicago Press, 2008.

Straparola, Giovan Francesco. *The Pleasant Nights.* Ed. and trans. Suzanne Magnanini. Toronto: Centre for Reformation and Renaissance Studies, 2015.

Truglio, Maria. *Italian Children's Literature and National Identity: Childhood, Melancholy, Modernity.* New York: Routledge, 2018.

Uther, Hans-Jörg. *The Types of International Folktales. A Classification and Bibliography. Based on the System of Antti Aarne and Stith Thompson.* Three volumes. Helsinki: Suomalainen Tiedeakademia, Academia Scientiarum Fennica, 2004.

Warner, Marina. *From the Beast to the Blonde: On Fairy Tales and Their Tellers.* New York: Farrar, Straus, and Giroux, 1994.

Zipes, Jack. "The Indomitable Giuseppe Pitrè." *Folklore* 120, no. 1 (2009): 1–18.

■ Biographical Notes

Luigi Capuana (1839–1915). A prolific author of realistic fiction for adults and major exponent of Sicilian *verismo* literature (with novels including *Il marchese di Roccaverdina* [The Marquis of Roccaverdina], 1901, and *Giacinta*, 1879). His many collections of original literary fairy tales for children show this author's intimate knowledge of the form and content of the orally transmitted tales of his home region; his fairy tales implicitly criticize both Sicilian social reality and the tiresome didacticism of the children's literature of that time. "Sunbeam" appeared in his first volume of fairy tales, *C'era una volta . . . Fiabe* (Once upon a time . . . fairy tales, 1882) and "Golden Feather" in *Il Raccontafiabe* (The tale teller, 1894).

Collodi (Carlo Lorenzini, 1826–90). A writer, journalist, and politician, he is forever remembered as the author of the children's novel *The Adventures of Pinocchio* (1883). Commissioned in 1875 with translating a collection of French fairy tales by Charles Perrault, Marie-Catherine d'Aulnoy, and Jeanne-Marie Leprince de Beaumont (the book in which his Tuscanized "Donkey Skin" first appeared), he shifted the emphasis of his work to literature for children. Collodi's translation of the title characters' names of Perrault's classic tales, such as Little Red Riding Hood (Cappuccetto Rosso) and Bluebeard (Barba-blu), were to remain the standard Italian versions, supplanting all earlier translations.

Domenico Comparetti (1835–1927). A classicist, field archaeologist, politician, and philologist. His *Novelline popolari italiane* (Popular Italian stories, 1875), which includes "The King's Son, a Pig," "The Pomegranates," and "Bad Pumpkin," is unusual among nineteenth-century collections of Italian folk tales because it includes tales from all over Italy translated by this scholar from the local dialect into standard Italian; only the first of three projected volumes was published. Although Comparetti's collection did not gain great popularity during the author's lifetime, Italo Calvino included many of these tales in his own celebrated collection *Italian Folktales* of 1956.

Cordelia (Virginia Tedeschi Treves, 1849–1916). A journalist and publisher and an author of plays, novels, short stories, and fairy tales, she used a pen name inspired by the favorite daughter of Shakespeare's *King Lear*. Although her first book, *Il regno della donna* (Woman's kingdom, 1876), was explicitly anti-feminist, her last, *Le donne che lavorano* (Women who work, 1916), asserts that women have the right to work for reasons other than financial necessity. Cordelia's patriotic outlook informs her 1894 collection *Piccoli eroi* (Little heroes), a publishing success that went through sixty-two editions and encouraged young people to perform their duty as patriots. Her two popular volumes of literary fairy tales, *Nel regno delle fate* (In the kingdom of the fairies, 1884) and *L'ultima fata* (The last fairy, 1909, in which "Prince Valorous's Doll" and "Fiery Eyes" appeared), although far more nuanced, also have a clear pedagogical intent that contrasts with the more whimsical and/or traditional tales of many of her contemporaries.

Gabriele D'Annunzio (1863–1938). One of the best-known writers of his time, he was a controversial yet influential author of poetry, prose, and drama (including *Il piacere* [*The Child of Pleasure*], 1889; *Laudi del cielo, del mare, della terra e degli eroi* [*In Praise of Sky, Sea, Earth, and Heroes*], 1899). He was also a political and military activist who, in his fifties, volunteered to fight in World War I, promoting an interventionist propaganda and drawing inspiration from Italian unification hero Giuseppe Garibaldi.

Though he never became a member of the Fascist party, he was among the first to sign the manifesto of fascist intellectuals in 1925 and was widely acclaimed as a fascist by Mussolini and his followers. He published the Abruzzese folk tales "The Doves" and "The Song of the Bloodied Ricotta" in literary magazines, and the literary fairy tale "The Borea's Daughter," written in his characteristic decadent style, in a collection of parables and short stories of 1914. The folklore of D'Annunzio's native region of Abruzzi is also featured in his better-known works of fiction, such as *Le novelle della Pescara* (The stories of Pescara, 1902) and the fairy-tale-like play *La figlia di Iorio* (*The Daughter of Jorio*, 1904).

Grazia Deledda (1871–1936). The only Italian woman to have received the Nobel prize in literature (1927). Her literary attention to her native island of Sardinia led critics to label her work as limited because of its regionalism. Her best-known novels include *Canne al vento* (*Reeds in the Wind*, 1913); *Elias Portolu* (1900); and *Cenere* (*Ashes*, 1904). The attachment to Sardinia led Deledda to studying the island's folklore, legends, and traditional tales, which she rewrote and transformed into more accessible literary forms. She wrote in standard Italian but, like other non-Tuscan Italian writers of that time period, experienced it as a second language (Sardinian was her mother tongue). "Our Lady of Good Counsel" and "The Three Talismans" were published in literary magazines; Deledda's Sardinian legends were collected into a volume and published years after her death, as *Fiabe e leggende* (Fairy tales and legends, 1994) and *Leggende sarde* (Sardinian legends, 1999).

Guido Gozzano (1883–1916). The best-known exponent of *crepuscolarismo* (the poetry of twilight, from the Italian *crepuscolo*), a literary movement marked by a quiet, ironic aesthetic and quotidian themes, the style of which influenced his literary fairy tales as well. He traveled to India in 1912 in hopes of finding a better climate for his failing health; during the same years that he was working on his major collection of poems, *I colloqui* (Dialogues), Gozzano published fairy tales in children's periodicals—especially the popular *Corriere dei piccoli*, where "Goldenfeather and Finestlead," "The Dance of the Gnomes," and "The Three Talismans" were published between 1909 and 1910. Collected in 1914 in *I tre talismani* (The three talismans) and in 1917 in *La principessa si sposa* (The princess is getting married), Gozzano's fairy tales remained popular throughout the twentieth century, going through some twenty editions.

Emma Perodi (1850–1918). A journalist, writer, and translator, she wrote realistic fiction for adults but is best known for her fantastic writing for children—especially the voluminous collection *Le novella della nonna* (Grandmother's tales), forty-five tales of magic told within a realistic frame narrative set in rural Tuscany, Perodi's native region, and published in five volumes between 1892 and 1893. "The She-Mule of Abbess Sofia," "Lavella's Stepmother," and "The Madonna's Veil" all appeared in this volume. Deeply attentive to the works of the Italian folklorists who were her contemporaries, and a personal friend of the Sicilian folklorist Giuseppe Pitrè—who wrote favorably about her work—Perodi wrote original literary creations shaped by the content and style of orally transmitted narratives, infused with popular Catholicism and superstition and influenced by genres such as the gothic and the feuilleton.

Yorick (Pietro Coccoluto Ferrigni, 1836–95). A lawyer, writer, journalist, translator from the French, and patriot, he fought alongside Garibaldi for the unification of Italy, both as Garibaldi's secretary and as a soldier. He was famous for his prodigious memory, and took his pen name, "Yorick figlio di Yorick" (Yorick, son of Yorick), from Shakespeare as used by Laurence Sterne. In 1891, he translated as *Il libro delle fate* (The book of fairies) Perrault's fairy tales of 1697; Perrault's "The Fairies," which Yorick translated as "Le fate"—missing from Collodi's 1876 translation of French tales—is drawn from Yorick's book and normally appears in Collodi's collection, without credit to its actual translator.